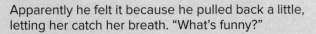

Apparently he felt it because he pulled back a little, letting her catch her breath. "What's funny?"

She could feel her cheeks heat. She hoped he thought it was the heat from the fireplace, although it wasn't that warm. "It's silly," she said, sounding as if she had to force the words out.

"Oh. That's okay. I always thought you were the most wildly beautiful woman I'd ever seen."

Wildly beautiful? Her heart slammed and began a rapid tap dance of delight. "I was just thinking..." She drew a breath and blurted it. Truth for truth. "I was just thinking I should have jumped your bones a long time ago."

The smile that spread over his face would have lit the arctic night brighter than the aurora. "Oh, I do like the sound of that."

With a gentle hand, he cupped her cheek and drew her in for another kiss. "Jump away," he murmured against her lips. "Anytime."

MISSING IN CONARD COUNTY

New York Times Bestselling Author

RACHEL LEE

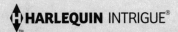
HARLEQUIN INTRIGUE®

Recycling programs
for this product may
not exist in your area.

ISBN-13: 978-1-335-64059-8

Missing in Conard County

Copyright © 2018 by Susan Civil Brown

Printed in U.S.A.

Rachel Lee was hooked on writing by the age of twelve and practiced her craft as she moved from place to place all over the United States. This *New York Times* bestselling author now resides in Florida and has the joy of writing full-time.

Books by Rachel Lee

Harlequin Intrigue

Conard County: The Next Generation

Cornered in Conard County
Missing in Conard County

Harlequin Romantic Suspense

Conard County: The Next Generation

Guardian in Disguise
The Widow's Protector
Rancher's Deadly Risk
What She Saw
Rocky Mountain Lawman
Killer's Prey
Deadly Hunter
Snowstorm Confessions
Undercover Hunter
Playing with Fire
Conard County Witness
A Secret in Conard County
A Conard County Spy
Conard County Marine
Undercover in Conard County
Conard County Revenge
Conard County Watch

Visit the Author Profile page at Harlequin.com.

CAST OF CHARACTERS

Allan Carstairs—County animal control officer and deputy. Former military special ops, recovering from invisible combat wounds and expressing his deep-rooted love of animals in his work. Finds Kelly Noveno wildly attractive.

Kelly Noveno—K-9 officer with the Conard County sheriff's office. She and Bugle, her dog, make an inseparable pair, almost as if they share their minds. She has been a police officer for nine years, following in the footsteps of her Puerto Rican father.

Jane Beauvoir—Eighteen years old, high school senior, chess club standout, wants to have a little fun in the last semester of school. Kidnapping victim.

Mary Lou Ostend—Eighteen years old, kidnapping victim, high school senior, also a member of the chess club as well as the debate club. Outgoing and difficult to manage. Her idea of fun runs a little on the wild side.

Chantal Reston—Eighteen years old, kidnapping victim, high school senior, hangs with the chess club but prefers being with animals. She has volunteered over the summer to work with Allan Carstairs. Bright and personable, and very smart.

Chapter One

The forecast called for a severe winter storm to move into Conard County, Wyoming, in the next two days, so animal control officer Allan Carstairs was out hunting for strays. By nightfall, the temperatures would be dropping rapidly, and while the storm itself wasn't moving fast, the cold was stampeding down on them. Subzero temperatures weren't good for animals that were used to warm homes and not used to dealing with Arctic weather. Al had seen cats with badly frostbitten paws and ears, and he would never forget the dog that needed a leg amputated. Nor would he ever forget the animals he had found frozen to death.

So when the weather was about to turn dangerous, he roamed the area outside town looking for strays, as well as a family of felines that a trucker had reported dropped by the roadside. A lot of people let their cats roam free, and any cat that didn't sense the changing weather as a reason to get home would be looking at trouble, even death. Then there were the dogs. The leash law didn't always keep them from escaping and having so much fun racing the countryside that they often didn't seem to realize danger was closing in.

At that moment he already had three annoyed cats in cages and a miniature schnauzer that appeared to be sad because he couldn't keep chasing a prairie dog.

Then he spied Misty. A beautiful golden retriever with a distinctive prance to her step, she seemed to be running in circles about a hundred yards inside the fence line of the Harris family ranch. He was surprised to see her so far out here. The Avilas had always been careful owners who tried not to let Misty slip her leash, but she was an accomplished escape artist. With the weather turning so bitter, perhaps one of the kids had let her out in the backyard without watching and she'd burrowed under the fence. Regardless, at the times she proved to be Houdini's reincarnation, Al usually picked her up within or near the city limits.

Al pulled his van onto the shoulder, grabbed a slipknot leash and climbed out. Misty had never been a problem to round up, so he expected her to come immediately when he called. Just after he slid off the seat and his feet hit the ground, he felt a light weight land on his shoulder and hang on. Regis, he thought, and smiled.

He closed the vehicle door so the animals would stay warm and gave thanks that the wind hadn't really started yet. Just the faintest of breezes to chill the air, and a tang that hinted at coming snow.

For the first time ever, Misty wasn't in a co-operative mood. As she raced around, she tossed some kind of toy in the air, and although she occasionally glanced at him when he called her, she kept right on playing, pausing only occasionally to paw at the ground before returning to her private game of catch.

"Hey, Misty," Al called. "Come on. Don't be a pain. Seriously."

Just then a sheriff's SUV pulled onto the opposite shoulder of the road. It bore a rack of lights and Conard County Sheriff painted in green on the tan background. K-9, Keep Your Distance was also labeled on the side. By that, before she even climbed out, Al knew it was Kelly Noveno.

She had apparently taken in the situation before she pulled over to approach him, and grinned as she climbed out. "Having a problem, Al?"

He had to grin back. Kelly was a wildly attractive woman to his way of thinking, but what he most liked about her was her sunny nature and readiness to tease. He also liked her dog, a

Belgian Malinois named Bugle for his slightly strange bark. Kelly left Bugle in her vehicle, however, and sauntered toward Al, her khaki uniform and jacket looking scarcely heavy enough to withstand the chilling air. "Misty giving you trouble?"

"She's in a mood, all right," Al agreed. Apparently, Kelly had had her own run-ins with the dog.

Kelly whistled, but Misty barely spared her a glance as she tossed her toy in the air and caught it.

"What in the world is she playing with?" Kelly asked.

"I've been wondering. Rawhide bone? Heck, she knows I wouldn't take that away from her."

Kelly chuckled. "She's teasing you." Then she turned to look at Al. "What in the dickens is that on your shoulder?"

Al didn't even have to glance. "That's Regis."

"That's a *squirrel*! You can't keep them for pets."

"I don't. Regis decides for himself. Sometimes he likes to ride shotgun. What can I tell you, Kelly? The squirrel has a mind of his own."

Al felt her staring but heck, what could he do about it? He'd rescued Regis as an abandoned baby, fed the animal until it was strong enough to take off into the woods and live the squirrel life. Except Regis kept coming back to visit.

"Now I've seen everything," Kelly muttered. "Someday I want to hear this story."

While Al wouldn't have minded spending the next day or two chatting with Kelly, there was still business to attend to. "Misty, get your butt over here now." This time there was an edge of impatience to his voice and Misty didn't miss it. She froze, looked at him, then came trotting over with her toy.

Al squatted down, ready to reward the dog with a good scratch and rub, but as Misty drew closer something inside him began to feel as chilly as the day.

"Kelly?"

"That's not rawhide," she said too quietly.

Al didn't answer. He waited until Misty snaked through the fence and came to a halt before him, dropping her toy and looking at him with a proud grin.

Al reached out, scratching her neck automatically as he looked down at the "present" she'd placed before him.

"Tell me that's not human," he said.

"I can't," Kelly answered, her voice unusually taut.

Their eyes met and Al knew they were both thinking of the same thing: the three high school girls who'd gone missing nearly a month ago.

"I'll get an evidence bag while you put the dog in your van," Kelly said. But he noted she walked to her SUV with a leaden step. All her natural vivacity had seeped away. She'd be calling for help, he thought, to try to learn where the dog found the bone. Before they were even certain.

"Yeah," Al said, speaking to the icy air. "Yeah." Then he stood, slipping the loose leash around Misty and leading her to the back of his truck.

"God," he told the dog, "I hope it's from a deer."

But he was very afraid it was not.

Chapter Two

Kelly Noveno rolled over in her bed with a groan, wishing she could knock the ringing phone off the hook and go back to sleep. Being a sheriff's deputy, she knew she couldn't do that even though she'd worked graveyard.

The night shifts ended in the wee hours with her being too wound up to sleep immediately. Inevitably while she worked she drank far too much coffee, and by the time she reached her snug little house near the edge of Conard City, she was wider awake than an owl. She unwound with recorded TV or music, and often didn't fall asleep until late morning.

Thus, no one should bother her this early. She'd made that much clear to the dispatcher. She and her dog, Bugle, must be allowed to sleep.

Right then Bugle, who was lying beside her on her rumpled queen-size bed, lifted his head and made a sound somewhere between a groan and a yawn.

"Yeah, me, too, boy." Except that as she pushed herself upright, she caught sight of the digital clock. Three in the afternoon was hardly early. If she were on shift tonight, she'd be getting up soon anyway.

"Hell," she muttered and stood in her red flannel pajamas, shoving her feet into warm slippers. "It's getting cold, Bugle." Even inside. The heat must be straining to keep up.

The phone jangled again, telling her it wasn't going to let her run away. Pushing her bobbed, straight black hair back from her face, she reached for the receiver and lifted it to her ear.

"Noveno," she answered, trying to sound alert and not groggy.

"Kelly, sorry to wake you," came the gravelly voice of the sheriff, Gage Dalton. She guessed her attempt to sound alert hadn't worked very well. "You found a car in the ditch along the state highway last night, didn't you?"

"Yeah." She closed her eyes, remembering. "About eleven o'clock. A trace on the tag said it belonged to Randy Beauvoir. I called and got no answer. Figured someone had picked the occupants up because it was so cold. No sign of any trouble, appeared to be a simple loss of control. I tagged it for tow because the rear end was dangerously near the edge of the traffic lane."

All of which had been in the report that she had typed at five that morning. Holiday weekend, lots of activity and lots of people not home. New Year's.

"I know you're probably still tired, but we need you to come in. Three girls are missing, last known to be in that vehicle. Their parents called us half an hour ago."

"Oh, God," she breathed. "I'll be there right away."

SHE FILLED BUGLE'S bowls with kibble and fresh water, then while he filled his belly she hurried into a fresh uniform. Which girls? The thought ran around inside her head like a hamster on a wheel.

Beauvoir. She didn't know the family well, but she'd met Randy and May's daughter briefly last fall during one of those "don't drink and drive" demos they put on every two years, showing the graphic aftermath of an accident. The girl, woman really, had been pretty and engaging and full of questions because she said she wanted to become an EMT. Eighteen and full of promise.

"Oh, God," she said aloud once more.

Bugle looked at her, forgetting his food.

"Go ahead and eat," she told him. "Who knows when this day will end." Or how.

SHE GRABBED SOME dry cereal from the cupboard, poured milk on it and ate it too quickly. A couple of power bars wound up in her jacket pockets after she donned her utility belt and gun.

Time to go.

Anyone who'd grown up here should know better than to wander away from a vehicle on a cold night. It was easy to get lost out there on those open expanses, and people ought to be aware how fast the cold could become fatal. She couldn't believe three high school women wouldn't be aware. It was possible, but she was more inclined to believe someone had offered them a ride.

It would have been considered criminal by most folks around here to leave someone with a broken-down vehicle in such cold.

But if someone had offered a ride, who? And where had the girls gone?

Her stomach kept taking one plunge after another as she drove to the office. Bugle whimpered in his caged-in backseat as if he felt her anxiety.

"It's okay, boy," she said, trying to sound calm. Okay? Less and less likely.

THE SHERIFF'S OFFICE was a beehive of activity, with barely enough space to move around other personnel. Conversation was quiet, weighted with gravity. It looked like the entire department's staff was here, along with the city police department under the direction of Chief Madison.

Before she heard a word, she recognized that a search was about to get underway.

"Kelly?"

Sheriff Gage Dalton waved her back to his office. She wormed her way through the crowd with Bugle, greeting everyone with a nod. She knew them all but there was no time for conversation, not now. Bad things were afoot.

Once inside the sheriff's office, she closed the door at his gesture and took the seat facing his desk. Every time Gage moved, pain flickered across his scarred face. The result of a long-ago bomb when he'd been with the DEA. While he tried to give the pain no quarter, she didn't mind his manual suggestion that she close the door herself. Why would she?

Bugle promptly sat beside her, ears pricked, at attention. He sensed something.

"Okay," he said. "You know we don't usually respond to a missing person report this quickly, especially not when the missing are legally all adults. Any one of those young women has the right to skip town and disappear."

She nodded. "But not right before high school graduation. Five months before college and vocational schooling or whatever."

"Exactly. Plus, how likely is it for three of them to pull a disappearing act and take nothing with them? One might, but not all of them. So we're going to start looking immediately. You found the car last night around eleven. We're not quite eighteen hours into this. Maybe a little more. I figure the first thing to do is start looking along the state highway. You said the car was facing west in the ditch?"

"Mostly. It might have spun out, I can't be sure, but I had the impression it was on its way back toward town. I also didn't see any tire skids, but that doesn't mean much as dark as it was. I didn't spend a whole lot of time looking, because there was no injury and no damage."

Gage nodded. "I've sent some people out to look at the highway for any kind of marks. So what have we got east along that road that might attract three young women on a holiday weekend night?"

Kelly was sure he knew the answer. "Rusty's Tavern. You want me to take Bugle out there?"

He nodded. "They'll be opening soon enough. Maybe one of the bartenders will remember them. Regardless, Bugle will know if they've been there."

He sure would, Kelly thought. "So what made their parents worry?"

"They knew the girls were going out last night. Each of their families thought they were staying at one of the other girl's homes. Apparently nothing definite had been arranged except a pajama party at one house or the other. By the time parents started worrying and calling each other, it was late and they all figured it wasn't that…simple."

It was so unlike the sheriff to hesitate over a word. She guessed he was as worried about the young women as anyone. As certain this wasn't going to end well.

"There's still hope," she said, rising as she realized he was done. "I'll head straight for the tavern. Do we have a target for my dog?"

"The parents are each bringing some clothing. Guess you'll have to wait until they get here."

"Or Bugle could smell the car interior. It's in the impound lot now, right?"

"He might get more scents than the girls."

She shook her head. "The parents aren't going to pick up a piece of their clothing without touching it. He's going to get multiple scents. One of the wondrous things about him is that he doesn't get them mixed up."

He put up a hand. "Whatever you think best." Glancing at the old wall clock to his right, he added, "Another half hour at least before anyone will be at Rusty's."

"I'll be there when they are." She paused. "We've got photos and personal data?"

"Not enough. Ask Sarah Ironheart. She may have been able to pull a digital copy of the yearbook. It won't be printed for another two months. Otherwise we're waiting for photos and all the rest from the parents."

She didn't want to meet the parents. Cowardly of her, she supposed, but right now all they could do, once they provided necessary information, was slow her down.

It wasn't that she didn't care. It was that she would care too much.

Sarah Ironheart sat at a desk near the front of the office, images scrolling across her monitor. A woman in her fifties, partly Native American, she had features that had worn the years well. Her long black hair, now streaked with gray, was caught in a ponytail on her neck, and the collar of her uniform shirt remained unbuttoned.

There was a chair beside the desk, and Kelly slid into it, waiting for Sarah to reach a pause point. "Damn it," Sarah said finally.

"What's wrong?"

"The yearbook editors haven't organized much of this file. I don't know how they'll get it finished in time to print it and put copies in students' hands by the end of the school year. Heck, some items aren't even in the total file yet, but in separate pieces."

Sarah leaned back in her chair. It was old and groaned as it tipped backward. "Coffee," she said as if it were the answer to everything.

"Want me to run across the street?"

Sarah cocked a dark eyebrow at her and smiled. "Trying to escape?"

Kelly half shrugged, feeling rueful. "I'd like to avoid the parents. Guess I can't."

"All of us should be that lucky. You still need a target. They're bringing them."

Kelly didn't even try to argue. Yeah, Bugle could pick up the girls' scents from the car, but they'd be much stronger on items of clothing. "Stay," she ordered Bugle. He waited, still as a piece of statuary, while Kelly stood. "How do you like your coffee?"

"Black. Thanks."

"No problem." The coffee bar was against the back wall, a huge urn that simmered all day long. The coffee was famously awful, but it carried a caffeine charge. What amused her, however, was that just in the time she'd worked here, she'd watched the addition of about seven types of antacids to the table behind the foam cups.

Velma, the dispatcher who had been with the department since the dinosaurs had roamed the earth, still smoked at her desk despite the no-smoking sign right over her head and made the coffee. No one ever complained. But now there was that row of antacids. Velma ignored it.

Kelly smothered a smile at the incongruities but poured Sarah her coffee. She'd like some herself, but she'd wait until she could get something that wouldn't hit her stomach like battery acid.

Sarah thanked her as she returned and handed over the coffee. Then she rubbed her neck once and returned to scanning the images on her screen. "It would help," she said quietly, "if all these photos were labeled by name. Or sorted by class."

"Still early days, huh?"

"For the yearbook, evidently."

Just then the front door opened and a blast of cold air could be felt all the way across the room. Kelly immediately recognized Allan Carstairs, the county's animal control officer. Although he was loosely attached to the sheriff's department, he seldom wore a uniform. Today a dark blue down parka with a hood covered him to below his narrow hips—funny that she could see those hips in her mind's eye—above jeans. Thermal long johns, she guessed. A staple for everyone during parts of the year. Like the insulated winter boots on his feet.

She watched him ease his way through the room, pausing to talk to some of the gathered deputies. At last he approached the spot where she sat with Bugle and Sarah.

"How's it going?"

"I guess we're going to see," she answered.

He nodded, his expression grim. Sharp angles defined his face, giving him a firm look that rarely vanished, even when he smiled. Gray eyes met hers, but right now the gray looked more like ice. It wasn't a warm color.

"Which three girls?" he asked.

Sarah spoke. "Jane Beauvoir, Mary Lou Ostend and Chantal Reston."

Kelly felt her heart squeeze. Jane had been the only one she'd met, but still. So young. So entitled to a future.

"Hell," said Al. "Chantal volunteered with me last summer."

"We need to get the rest of the K-9 units in here," Gage suddenly called from the hallway that led to his office in the back. "Where the hell is Cadel Marcus? Jack Hart? What kind of search can we run without the dogs?"

"A sloppy one," Kelly muttered. Bugle eyed her quizzically.

Impatience grew in Kelly. She wanted to get on with it, find out if the girls had been seen at the roadhouse last night. If so, there might be a clue about who had picked them up. Or might have. At this point, however, it had clearly been no simple offer of a ride home.

The door opened again, this time for longer and letting in more icy air as the fathers of the three girls arrived. Randy Beauvoir entered first, followed by Kevin Ostend and Luis Reston. Kelly knew all three of them by sight, but only vaguely as she'd never had any business with them or their families.

She rose to her feet just as Gage reappeared and greeted the three men. They looked tense, worried, even a touch fearful. "Come back to the conference room," Gage said. "You've got the pictures? The clothing?"

The men nodded and Gage turned. "Kelly?"

"Coming."

Velma's scratchy voice suddenly penetrated the murmur of quiet voices. "Boss? Connie Parish says they need some help with crowd control. Word is getting around and folks are gathering near where the car was found to start their own searches."

Gage cussed. "Send ten men out there before they trample any evidence. Get ten volunteers. I got some business here first, then I'll go out there, too."

"I'll go," said Al Carstairs. He might be the animal control officer, but he had the physical stature to be intimidating, and the military bearing to go with it.

Velma looked around. "Nine more?"

Before she could see who went, Kelly and Bugle were being ushered into the conference room. In the relative quiet once the door closed behind them, the room filled with a different atmosphere. Fear. Worry. Even some anger. These fathers were like rifles that didn't know where to point.

"We're helping with the search," Randy Beauvoir said.

"I never thought you wouldn't. But I need Deputy Noveno here to give Bugle his target scents, and I want pictures of your daughters to go out with her, and with damn near everyone else. We're going to digitize the photos. They'll be on every cell phone in the county, okay? And TV, as well. But first things first."

A SHORT WHILE LATER, after a quick stop at Maude's diner to get a tall, hot latte, with her truck heater blasting, Kelly and Bugle headed east out of town with evidence bags holding part of the girls' clothing and photocopies of the full-size portraits. Even as she was driving she heard her cell phone ding, and figured it was probably the digital photos with background info.

It was beginning to hit her. She'd found the vehicle that had been carrying the girls only last night. Shouldn't some instinct have kicked in? Made her look inside the car, study the ground around for signs of a scuffle? Anything?

But the scene hadn't struck her that way. Once she knew the occupants were gone, that even their purses had vanished, there seemed to be nothing to worry about. No one injured, because if they had been they would have been on their way to the hospital and her radio should have been crackling with information.

It had been quiet, dark. People misjudged and went into ditches all the time, especially on cold nights where even a small patch of black ice could cause loss of control. She hadn't seen or felt any ice, but that didn't mean it hadn't been there when the car ran off the road.

But without any damage to the car or any obvious sign of foul play, there was really nothing she could do except get the vehicle towed when she couldn't get ahold of the owner.

Randy Beauvoir and his wife had been in Laramie for the weekend. They'd come home midday today, Randy had told her and the sheriff. They'd received Kelly's voice mail but hadn't immediately worried. No messages suggested the girl was in trouble. Probably at a friend's house for the night, as discussed. They'd get the car out of impound later.

But then Chantal's family had phoned, and the dominoes started tumbling. The girls weren't at one of their houses. Their families had no idea where they might be. Kelly's message about the car had suddenly struck them as a blinding warning flare.

The early winter night had begun conquering the landscape. Bright floodlights warned her of the approaching accident scene. She felt ill to the pit of her stomach. As she passed the cordoned-off area where the car had been found and crowds were beginning to gather, all she could hope was that somebody at Rusty's would give her a clue.

THE GRAVEL PARKING lot was clear of all but one vehicle, an aging pickup truck. Neon signs in the windows didn't yet shimmer with life and wouldn't until Rusty officially opened his doors.

She knew Rusty. She'd been called a number of times to help when some customers grew rowdy. Rusty did a better job than most of keeping it under control, but sometimes even he needed help. Roadhouses farther out had more problems, but here only ten miles out of town, the clientele seemed less likely to want to tussle, especially with the law. Most nights people came, drank and danced to local live music, and peace ruled, if not quiet.

This was the place that drew the patronage of local couples as much as local cowboys, and while she doubted anyone would think it wise for an unescorted woman to come here, three teens should have been safe. Older folks would have kept an eye on them, and Rusty would have served them soft drinks.

The door was unlocked. She pulled the tarnished brass handle and the ancient entry squeaked open. Inside the lighting was dim. The table candles in their squat hurricane lantern holders hadn't been lit.

Rusty was behind the long bar, polishing it with a rag. Directly across the large room from him, across the big dance floor, was a stage still holding band equipment.

"Hey, Rusty," she said as she and Bugle entered. "How's business?"

"Pretty good, but it always is on a holiday weekend. Tonight we'll be damn near empty. Can I help you, Kelly?"

He was a tall, lean man who always looked as if he needed to eat more of his own sandwiches. A gray moustache curled around the corners of his mouth.

"Have you heard about the three girls who've gone missing?"

Rusty's watery blue eyes widened. "No. Is that why you're here?"

She nodded and opened the brown envelope she'd brought with her, the one that held the eight-by-ten photos of each girl. She recited their names as she pulled them out. "Jane Beauvoir, Chantal Reston and Mary Lou Ostend. All high school seniors. We found their car in a ditch about five miles west of here just last night. No sign of them anywhere."

"Jeez," Rusty said, leaning toward the photos as if his old eyes needed some magnification. Reaching up with one hand, he turned on a bright light over the bar. Kelly blinked.

"Anyone else here yet?" she asked, even though it didn't feel like it.

He shook his head. "We don't open for another hour. Not much to do before then." He picked up the photos one by one and studied them.

"They were here last night," Rusty said slowly. "Seems like they might have showed up a little after eight. Early. I hardly noticed because we were already full. Holiday," he said again as if in explanation.

"All three?"

"I do believe so."

"They hang out with anyone?"

He shook his head. "They sat at that table over there—" he pointed "—and drank enough diet soda to float a battleship." He lifted his gaze. "No alcohol, I swear."

She nodded. "Can I let Bugle sniff around while we talk?"

"Go for it, although how he's going to smell squat over the stale beer and fried chicken beats me."

She didn't argue or explain, but squatted down and pulled the three evidence bags from her pocket. One by one she let Bugle sniff them, then said, "Seek." He was off.

Straightening again, she pulled out her cell phone and hit the record button. "I'm taping this, okay? Just in case you mention something that winds up being important to us. All right by you?"

"Happy to do it," he answered. His gaze had wandered over to the table where he said the girls had been sitting. "Damn it, Kelly, they're so young and were just having fun. Haven't heard that much giggling since my own school days."

Then he paused and looked at her. "I didn't

pay close attention, though. I wish I had. I'm sorry. We were busy. All they were doing was sitting and drinking cola. Oh, yeah, and they ordered a BLT to share. That was it. I didn't see anything wrong so I wasn't staring."

She nodded. "I understand. Anything at all catch your attention? Did one of them dance with anyone?"

He scratched his head and closed his eyes, pondering. "Dance? I think I saw two of them dance together. Line dancing. Nobody feels awkward if they don't have a partner, you know?"

"I know. So that was it?"

"Maybe not," he said after another minute. "They're pretty. I saw some guys wander by to talk with them, but they didn't stay." His eyes popped open and met hers intently. "My opinion, if you want it…"

"Everything you've got."

"Those girls weren't looking for trouble of any kind. Now, I've had people their age in here before, skating the line of being unwise. Trying to get someone to buy them a beer, wanting to dance with anything in pants. It happens. These girls were different. It was like they were having a private party and everything else was background."

Kelly tipped her head a little. "Unusual?"

"For that age. I was impressed. Must have good mamas."

Kelly wouldn't know about that. Turning, she saw Bugle sitting patiently upright beside the table Rusty had pointed out. Yup, they'd been there.

"Seek," she told him again. Then the trail became more winding. It wandered out onto the dance floor, approached the bar, headed down the hall to the ladies' room, then back to the table. "Find," she urged him, envisioning the evening the three girls had spent here.

He lowered his head and wound up at the front door. They'd left.

She looked again at Rusty. "So…nothing concerned you. You didn't feel like getting out your baseball bat?" She'd seen him swing that thing once. It put a quick end to most arguments.

"I wish I could tell you something. Nothing got me concerned enough to really pay attention. Nothing raised my hackles. But I'll keep thinking on it. Dang, those poor girls. If the car was in the ditch I don't suppose they ran away."

"They didn't get far if they wanted to." Reluctantly, she turned off the recorder and slipped the photos back into the envelope. Then she passed him her business card, needlessly since he certainly knew her and how to call the department. It just made her feel like she was actually doing something. "In case," she said.

"In case," he agreed. "Can I post some photos?"

"They should be on everyone's cell phone

soon, but if you want some copies to put up, I'll let the office know."

He nodded slowly. "Maybe someone saw something I didn't. I'll tell everyone to check their phones tonight."

"And I'll get you some posters. It's early days yet, Rusty."

"Forty-eight hours, isn't that what they say?"

Her nod was short, wishing she could deny it.

"You never know," Rusty called after her as if to be reassuring. "They could be somewhere safe."

"Sure. Thanks for your help. Someone else might come round." Because they were all going to get dizzy running in circles trying to find these young ladies. Every step would be retraced a hundred times.

Damn!

Chapter Three

Al Carstairs stood by the roadside as the crowd grew around the yellow police tape. Nobody was wanted inside that sacred circle yet except the crime scene techs.

The ground beside the road, apart from being winter-hard and covered with bits of sprayed gravel, wasn't going to yield much, he thought. Even the grass in the ditch, long since in winter hibernation, could present only broken stalks.

But nothing was going to be overlooked. If they could find any sign the girls had been picked up, or if they'd wandered off into the night, they had to locate it.

For his own part, he stepped back and began to walk along the pavement. Not even rubber skid marks to indicate the girls had tried to stop in a hurry, or swerved to avoid something.

Squatting, safely within the orange cones around which light traffic was being directed by cops wearing bright yellow vests, he scanned every inch of pavement.

He couldn't imagine why the driver hadn't tried to stop. Ice? Possible, but then the shoulder should have been torn up by the locked tires.

Something wasn't right. Then it struck him.

He stood and wondered whom he should talk to. Then he saw Kelly Noveno's SUV headed his way. Kelly. She was a smart one, and he trusted her judgment. He knew damn near everyone in the sheriff's office, but not in the same the way he knew Kelly. His animal control job often brought them together because of Bugle. Yeah, there were others he trusted as much or more, but none of them were out here right now.

How could a car go off the road without the driver trying to stop it? How could someone abscond with three high school girls? Rudolph the Reindeer's nose couldn't have blinked more brightly in his mind.

Kelly pulled over, inside the cones, then climbed out and approached him. "Nothing?" she asked, waving at the crime techs.

"Not from them yet. Kelly… I had a nuts idea. Tell me I'm crazy and I'll shut up."

She tilted her head. A tall woman, she didn't have to look up very high to meet his gaze. Dark snapping eyes. Full of vigor.

She nodded slowly. "Talk to me, Al. So far I'm coming up dry. Rusty thought they were the most well-behaved teens he'd ever had in his tavern, not even remotely looking for trouble. He said they seemed to be having a private party among the three of them."

Al nodded, but felt anxiety running along his nerve endings. So the girls hadn't been looking for trouble. That didn't mean they hadn't found it. It just meant it had been harder to find.

"What are you thinking?" Kelly pushed.

"No skid marks."

"Black ice."

He shook his head. "They still would have braked, and if they'd been braking to try to avoid going in the ditch or to avoid an obstacle, the shoulder would be torn up. Frozen as it is, it would have shown some tire marks. So they didn't brake."

He saw realization dawning on her face. "You're suggesting they weren't conscious? At least the driver?" Then she paused and swore. "Rusty said some guys passed their table briefly and chatted with them."

"Enough time," he answered.

She nodded, her expression growing even grimmer. She squatted to take a look at the pavement for herself, then straightened to study the shoulder once again. "Okay, I'm heading back to the tavern. Maybe Rusty knows who some of those guys were."

"I'm coming with you."

Animal control was part of the sheriff's department, but Al wasn't a standard deputy. It wasn't exactly pro forma for him to go along on an investigation, but everyone else was busy at the moment, and Kelly thought extra brains could always be useful.

"Let's go."

Despite the traffic hang-up around the scene, they got through quickly and were soon whizzing toward Rusty's. Bugle, in his backseat cage, knew Al so didn't seem disturbed by the addition of another person.

"It makes sense," Kelly said, although she didn't want to believe it.

"That someone could have drugged them? It's a wild hair, Kelly. It just popped into my head and wouldn't let go."

"I get it, but it still makes sense. Some guys stopped by their table to talk. And frankly, Al, considering these were young women out on a holiday weekend for some fun, they left Rusty's awfully early. I found the abandoned car just before eleven. When you were that age, did you call it a night that early?"

"No," he admitted. "Never."

"Exactly. No one was waiting for them, it was New Year's, all the parties would have been the night before. It's entirely possible that someone slipped something into their drinks and when they started to feel odd they decided to go home."

And that was crossing a lot of bridges with very little evidence, she thought. But it *did* make sense. She had to at least find out what guys were talking to them, if Rusty knew. Then she could interview them to see what more she could learn.

"Anyway," she said more to herself than him, "I didn't think of trying to track these guys down when Rusty mentioned them because he made it seem like it was all brief and in passing. I think I ought to kick my own butt. I should have gotten suspicious right then."

"Cut yourself some slack," Al said. "Three girls together at a table. A lot of men would stop by, get the brush-off and move on. Normal behavior. Nothing to stand out."

"Except the girls are missing." She clenched her teeth until her jaw ached, and when she turned into Rusty's parking lot she sprayed gravel.

She climbed out, leaving Bugle in the car with a cracked window and the heater on. Ten minutes. If this took longer, she'd come out and get her dog.

She slammed the SUV door emphatically, glanced at the watch on her wrist and marched toward the door, hardly aware that Al was on her heels.

Just then she was feeling awfully stupid. Stupid, and cold as the night nipped at her cheeks and the wind tossed her hair. She hoped the missing young women were safe and warm.

But she seriously doubted they were.

A COUPLE OF people had evidently showed up for work. A woman of about forty, wearing a leather fringed skirt, was making her way around the tables, lighting the hurricane lanterns. A younger man used a push broom on the dance floor, clearing off any remains of last night's revels.

"Already?" Rusty said, arching a brow as he pushed a spout into the top of a whiskey bottle.

"Some thoughts occurred," Kelly said. "Al?"

Rusty looked at him. "I know you. The animal control guy. What's up?"

Al unzipped his jacket halfway. Rusty didn't keep the place overwarm, but warm enough that winter gear could be suffocating. "Al Carstairs. I've got just a couple of questions, if you don't mind."

"You looking for these girls, too? I'm not surprised. Half the county will be out there tomorrow. Wish it wasn't so late right now. So, what can I do you for?"

"There's a chance the girls, or at least the driver, were unconscious when they went off the road."

Rusty straightened until he was stiff. He looked toward the table where the young women had been sitting just the night before. "Yeah?" he said hoarsely.

"Not sure," Kelly hastened to say. "Just an idea we're looking into."

Rusty nodded. He turned his attention again to Al. "What do you want to know?"

"You said some men stopped by their table. Do you remember who?"

Kelly had turned on her cell phone recorder and placed it on the bar so Rusty would know she was recording. He looked at it briefly.

"I gotta think," he said. "Like I told Kelly, I wasn't paying close attention. There was nothing that made me think anything was going on except three kids drinking soda together and having a great time. Two brunettes, one bottle blonde."

"Chantal," Al interpolated. "The blonde. Turned eighteen two months ago. Hard worker. Never heard a complaint out of her about cleaning my kennels. She did love the animals, though. Talked about wanting to be a veterinarian."

Kelly drank in the facts, but wondered why Al felt it necessary to add them. To make Chantal seem more real to Rusty?

Maybe it had worked, because Rusty's frown turned really dark. "Yeah, she stood out. The other two were cute, too. Having a great time together."

"Jane wanted to be an EMT," Kelly volunteered. Without another word, Rusty leaned his hands on the bar and looked down, eyes closed. He appeared to be straining to remember the night before. After a minute, he looked up and called, "Martha? Those teen girls who were here last night?"

The woman, carrying her electric match, came over to the bar. Her fading red hair was caught neatly into a netted bun, and the harsh sun and wind had given her a few wrinkles around her eyes and mouth. "Blonde and two brunettes? Youngest gals in here? Yeah. They was cute."

"Some guys talked to them. I can't remember who. Maybe one was Don Blevin?"

Martha shook her head. "I saw a couple of guys. Let me think. Dang, Rusty, we had so many folks in here last night."

"I know," he answered heavily.

Martha's eyes suddenly widened and she looked at Kelly's uniform. "Is these the girls what's missing? Oh my God…"

"That's why it's so important that you tell us everything you can remember," Kelly said. "Everything. How did they get their drinks? Who talked to them? Did anything seem…off?"

Understanding dawned on Martha's face. "You think they coulda been drugged?"

"We're just theorizing here," Al hastened to say. "Call it a wild idea. We don't know. We *can't* know."

Martha nodded, her expression as sober as a

judge's. Then she turned her head a bit. "Jack, you got a minute?"

Shortly they were joined by the young man who'd been pushing the broom.

"Jack knows the younger set," Martha explained. "Who was them guys who stopped by the table of the three teen girls who was sitting over there last night. You know the guys?" She pointed at the table.

Jack's forehead creased and a lock of greasy hair fell over his forehead to make a small curl. "Sure. First it was Hal Olsen."

Kelly had pulled out her patrol book and wrote quickly despite recording all this. "Tell us about Hal?"

Jack shrugged. "He ain't nothin'. Maybe thirty. His wife left him two months ago and he's pretty much been living here. He likes to get hisself a dance with the pretty women. The girls didn't want any so he walked away."

"And after that?" Al asked.

"He got hisself a dance with Margot Eels. Pretty enough so I don't think he was feeling dissed."

"Who else?" Al asked.

Jack worked his mouth as if it would help his brain to think. "Art Mason. He's another regular. Drinks too much sometimes and Rusty has to cut him off, but I don't think he was sober when he talked to them gals." He flashed a faint smile.

"Was kind of weaving. The gals laughed a bit after they sent him on his way. I think he landed in a chair near the dance floor. Then there was Keeb Dustin. Everybody knows the guy. Got hisself the service station east of town."

"Never causes trouble," Martha agreed. "He comes one night a week, either Friday or Saturday. He occasionally hits on someone, but not in a way that makes them complain."

"Anyone else?" Al asked.

"Don't know," Jack said. Martha shrugged.

"How'd the girls get their drinks?" Al asked.

"I brought 'em," Martha said promptly. "Fill up my tray with drinks at the station there, then pass them around to the tables. Keeps the bar from getting too crowded."

Kelly looked at Al for the first time. She saw awareness in his gray eyes, too. "Martha? You ever set your tray down with drinks on it?"

"Have to," she answered. "Gotta rearrange those bottles and glasses so I don't spill them all over anyone."

"But you're watching it every minute?"

"No," Martha answered. "People wanna talk. That's part of my job."

Kelly's stomach sank like a stone. So it was possible the girls had been slipped a drug. "How about," she said slowly, "you three make a list of everyone you can remember was in here last night. I'll pick it up tomorrow."

All three were agreeable, but Rusty looked positively dour. "I can't keep my eye on everything," he said to Kelly.

"Of course you can't, Rusty," she said reassuringly. "You folks have been a ton of help. And as for this suspicion, it's just that. Keep it quiet. We don't know that anything happened here at all. We just need every bit of information we can find."

Outside in the cold night, hearing Bugle call to her from the slightly open window of her truck, Kelly tried to keep her step steady as she walked toward him. Other cars were arriving now, but the flow wasn't heavy. Most of the interest would be down the highway around the crime scene. Folks had gathered to help, or out of curiosity. Who could say? But the crowd, the tape, the lights would draw attention. Wetting one's whistle could wait a short while.

When she laid her hand on the door of her vehicle, however, she froze. Then she tilted her head back and looked up at the amazingly clear star-filled sky.

She hoped that somewhere out in those desolate spaces there weren't three young women looking up at the stars with dead eyes.

Al was suddenly beside her, touching her arm. "Nobody would go to all that trouble just to kill them."

She lowered her gaze to his face. "Maybe that's even worse."

"Then we have to keep going, push as hard as we can."

"Yeah." Her answer was short, but she squared her shoulders and shook off the despair that wanted to overtake her. They had to find them as quickly as possible. Somewhere there had to be an essential clue.

She just wished she knew where to look beyond this tavern.

"Let's go," she said. "We have at least three guys to track down and get someone out to them for interviews."

The car felt too hot when she climbed in, but a glance at the dash thermometer told her it was sixty-eight. A good temperature for Bugle. He woofed a welcome.

As soon as Al was in the passenger seat with the door closed, she reached for her radio. Velma's scratchy voice answered.

"Hey, Velma," Kelly said. "Is Gage around?"

"Yeah, in the conference room working out a plan for tomorrow's search. You need him?"

"Please." She waited a couple of minutes, then heard the sheriff's gravelly voice.

"What's up, Kelly?"

"We were talking to employees at the tavern. I need someone to hunt up three guys and question them about the interactions they had with the three missing girls last night at Rusty's." Flipping open her notebook, she read the names to Gage.

"Slower," he said. Then, "Okay, got it. I know two of them. I'll send some deputies out to talk to them. Thanks, Kelly. Good work."

"Thank Al Carstairs. He's been a great help."

"I will. Are you coming in?"

"Absolutely. We need to talk in person." No way was she going to put the drug theory on the air. God knew how many police band radios would pick it up. The names of the men she wanted questioned didn't worry her. They'd come up at the tavern and she was sure they were about to be shared with the evening's early customers.

Gage's laugh was dry. "See you shortly."

Kelly looked down at the tall cup of latte she'd allowed to grow as cold as the interior of the truck. "I think I'm going to take a brief break. I need some coffee to get through this night."

"I'll join you," Al answered. "It'd make some good time to run over what we just learned."

Bugle seemed to quietly woof his agreement.

Yeah, they needed to do that, Kelly thought as she put the SUV in gear, swung a wide circle and drove back onto the state highway. Time to think it all over. You could get only so far just by picking up the puzzle pieces. Sooner or later you had to try to put them together.

She glanced sideways at Al, and out of no-where came the unbidden wish that this would be a social coffee. Nope. They could be friends but they had to remain professional or risk making a mess. If he was even interested.

Besides, the only thing that mattered tonight was three missing girls, girls who might be terrified out of their minds. Girls who might be suffering.

Girls who might be dead.

THE CROWD AT the accident scene had thinned out. She paused long enough to let Al jump out to get his truck while she surveyed the faces that looked so odd in the arc lamps. It was getting later and colder, and evidently people thought nothing more would happen tonight. Overhead the county's two choppers were flying a search pattern with bright spotlights sweeping over barren fields.

Fifteen minutes later, she pulled into a parking spot in front of the City Diner, also known as Maude's, and through the diner windows scanned the interior. Al pulled in beside her and climbed out, coming over to her window. She opened her door halfway but didn't get out.

"No discussion here tonight," she remarked. The place was jammed full.

"I'll run in and get the coffee, then," Al said. "Nobody will badger *me* with questions. Think

Gage would like some? And if so how does he like it?"

"Are we going to offend Velma?" she asked almost absently. Her thoughts were far away, reaching out into the frigid, empty night, trying not to imagine horrible things.

"Do we care? Gage."

"Yeah, he always wants his black, I think."

"You?"

"The biggest hot latte Maude makes."

"I'll see you at the office, then."

She listened to her door squeak as she closed it. The thing always squeaked when it was cold. She glanced over her shoulder at Bugle and figured he was probably starting to get desperate for some room to move. He tolerated the caging part of the job, but he was naturally very active.

Smothering a sigh, she threw her truck into gear and drove it the half block to the sheriff's offices. Across the street was the courthouse square, where Bugle could run a few laps and deposit his business. She let him out, then grabbed a plastic bag to clean up after him. He was good about that, always doing his business near her so she didn't have to run around needlessly.

When he was done she dumped the bag in the trash can, then turned to cross the street to the office. She saw Al just about there carrying a tray and a big brown bag with handles from the diner.

"That looks like more than coffee," she remarked as they met at the door. Since his hands were full, she reached out to open it.

"Maude's clearing some things out for the night. I hope everyone likes pie."

"Maude's pies? I think half this county would crawl across hot sand to get to one."

He gave a short laugh. Relief. They needed something to leaven the horror.

Inside, the office was much quieter than it had been earlier. Only four officers sat at desks. Probably a great many deputies had been sent home to rest up for a search tomorrow. Any others might be out protecting the crash site. Even Velma had vanished, a very rare thing.

Al lined up four pies on the table near the coffee. They were going to make plenty of people happy in the morning. Right now, he cut into an apple pie and served himself the wedge on a paper plate. "Hey, guys," Al said to the others, "help yourself to the pie. What would you like, Kelly?"

For the first time in hours she remembered that all she had eaten was a bowl of cereal.

"There's apple, blueberry, mincemeat and cherry."

The thought of any of them made her mouth water. "Apple would be great."

Gage had apparently heard their voices because he came out of the back, thanked them for the coffee and dug into the mincemeat pie.

He led them to the conference room, where maps covered the table. "Planning for tomorrow," he said as he eased into a high-backed chair. "Now, what's going on with these three guys—who are being interviewed right now, I believe—and what didn't you want to mention on the radio?"

"I'll let Al tell you," Kelly said. "He thought of it."

"A wild hair," Al said yet again.

"It didn't sound so wild after we went back to the tavern and talked to Martha. Go on." She spooned a small bit of apple pie into her mouth, to make it clear she wasn't talking, and wished only that she could savor it as all of Maude's pies deserved savoring. Right now, as knotted with worry as she was, it might as well have been ash.

"Well," Al said slowly, "I was looking at the highway and shoulder. Everyone thinks the girls skidded."

"And you don't?" Gage asked.

"Not likely. If they'd braked, even if they didn't leave tread marks on the pavement because of black ice, they'd have chewed up the shoulder, frozen or not. That car is too old to have anti-lock brakes, so there should have been some sign."

Gage swallowed a mouthful of mincemeat,

followed by some coffee. "You're right, and at last report from the scene, they're not finding any clues as to why the car went off the road." He paused, his dark gaze intent. "That doesn't mean they won't."

"I know. I'm not a crime scene tech. Hell, I'm only half a deputy."

"I beg to differ, but go on."

"Well, it was like a light going on in my head. Why wouldn't they brake when going off the road? Maybe they were unconscious or seriously drunk on soft drinks."

Gage sat up a little straighter and put his paper plate and plastic fork down. Pain rippled across his face but it didn't remain. The frown did.

"You think they were drugged? Before they left the tavern?"

Al shook his head. "I don't know. I can't prove it."

"But," Kelly interjected, "Martha, who served their drinks, said she often puts her drinks tray down, either to rebalance it or because people want to chat. In other words, nobody watched those girls' drinks every second between bar and table."

"Nobody would think it necessary," Gage murmured. He'd forgotten his pie and his coffee and rubbed his chin. "The problem around here is that people know one another. It wouldn't occur to them to question the trustworthiness of a neighbor. Over time, they've sometimes had to, but by and large those are considered isolated incidents, nothing to worry about. Most people still don't lock their doors. We've grown, it's no longer a place where everyone knows everyone else, but the attitudes are still mired in an earlier time. We don't even imagine anyone would drug three young women. And yet, it's entirely possible we've got a sicko running around. As the old sheriff, Nate Tate, liked to say, 'This county's going to hell in a handbasket.' Not really, but change has been happening for a while."

He fell silent for a few beats. "Drugs. Damn it all to hell, I can see it and it would explain a lot."

"They left the bar early, too," Kelly said. "Kids that age don't end their partying around ten o'clock. I imagine they started to feel unwell."

"Probably so." He shook his head, then reached for his coffee. "Okay, then. Things just got even more complicated. If they were drugged, it had to be someone who didn't stand out at Rusty's place or we'd have heard about him by now."

He eyed Kelly. "In short, one of our neighbors."

Twenty minutes later, Gage sent them both on their way. "You need to rest up for tomorrow. It's going to be a long, cold day."

"I want to know what kinds of answers we get from those three guys," Kelly argued.

"Unless one of them confesses, it'll hold till

morning. Besides, we've got a team going out there to try to speak to everyone who was at the bar last night. You might as well get your sleep. If anything breaks, I'll let you know."

Kelly had to be content with that. She really didn't know what else she could do out there.

"Tips should start coming in," she remarked. "I can man the phones."

"There are already four deputies out there doing exactly that. Take Bugle home."

Out of arguments, Kelly obeyed. Al walked out with her but only around the corner to where she was parked. He needed to collect his vehicle from down the street in front of the diner. Kelly watched her breath blow clouds, and couldn't help but notice it was growing colder. Of course it was. It was night.

And the young women...

She truncated the thought. Running it ceaselessly through her head wasn't going to improve anything. With the rising sun at least they could search, maybe stop to ask questions at homesteads that weren't too far out.

Right now...right now they just needed to wait for word to spread. Then would come the tips, mostly useless.

But at the moment... She just shook her head.

Al spoke as they neared her vehicle. "You going to be okay?"

Her head snapped around and she stopped walking. "Why wouldn't I be?"

He faced her directly. "I'm a combat vet, Kelly. I know about second-guessing, delayed reactions and sometimes shutdowns. This has got you upset and worried. You give a damn. You're not just going to go home and turn on the TV to some romantic comedy or suspense movie."

No, she wasn't. Everything inside her was knotted with frustration and worry. She probably wouldn't sleep worth a damn. "Sometimes you just have to endure. Get through it."

He nodded. "I know. I'm just saying…" He turned his head away. "Forget it. You need an ear, I'm available. This is probably going to eat you alive until we find those girls."

She figured it probably would. She just hoped they found the young women soon and found them unharmed.

Then she and Bugle headed home for what she anticipated was going to be a very long night.

Chapter Four

Bugle found the first scent. At the scene of the accident, he nosed the ground and followed it to the highway's edge. There he stopped.

It wasn't a good sign, but everyone hoped Bugle was wrong or that some kind person had picked the girls up.

Or at least everyone *tried* to hope. If the girls had been given a ride by a friendly person, surely they would have called home by now. The silence had become terrifying for their families, and for everyone else.

Despite Bugle's following the scent to the road, no one even thought of calling off the search. They might have walked down the pavement, the cold might have weakened their scents. Regardless, there was no way they'd stop this search, whatever the dog might indicate.

Cadel Marcus, part-time deputy and dog trainer, joined Kelly at roadside with his K-9,

Dasher. "I'm with you. Those girls didn't wander off over the fields. No scents on the far side of the road either."

"We still have to look. Someone could have left them farther along."

"Maybe." He nodded to Al, who joined them. "How's the dog-catching business?"

"I get most of them home. Say, if you want a shepherd mix to train, I have one whose owners are apparently fed up with his wanderlust."

Cadel nodded slowly. "Wonder what they're doing to make him run. Yeah, I'll take a look at him later. See what kind of potential he has."

Al's voice turned dry. "He's working on a teddy bear right now."

That drew a laugh from Cadel and even a very sober Kelly smiled.

The helicopters flew above again, having taken off as soon as the light was good enough to see the ground below. The searchers, civilian and police, were divided up into about ten groups and spaced out along both sides of the highway, on either side of the wreck scene. Between the rough ground and brush, they had to move slowly in order to avoid missing something important.

At this point few of the searchers hoped to find the girls. Now most of them were hoping for a clue. An item of clothing, a shoe, a purse, anything that might indicate the direction in which they had disappeared.

To Kelly's dismay, Bugle didn't seem particularly interested. She knew that he could pick up a scent from quite a long distance, either on the ground or in the air above his head. His boredom was as loud as a paid infomercial.

No girls around here.

Her gloved hand tightened on his leather leash, and she had to force herself to pay attention anyway. Scents were harder to detect in the cold, she reminded herself. Bugle might need to get closer.

But at that point, she didn't know if finding the girls out here after a long cold night would necessarily be a good thing.

Damned if they did, damned if they didn't. Never had that phrase seemed more apt.

THE GROUND SEARCH was called off for the night. Not a thing had been found. Kelly dragged herself back to her snug little house on the edge of town, a place that needed far more attention than she gave it. All her plans for fixing it up had kind of washed away in the reality of being a deputy covering so much territory for such a relatively small department. Oh, they had enough people to cover the routine, and even a group of investigators and a crime scene unit, but when something blew up, it was all hands on deck.

Something had blown up.

She fed Bugle some extra kibble and treated him to some chicken livers she boiled for him from a frozen stash she kept. He'd had a long, cold day, too, and gratefully scarfed it all down.

For herself she did nothing but make a pot of coffee because she needed something hot, fast. Then she collapsed in her easy chair, pinching the bridge of her nose to try to stave off a headache. The sense of hopelessness seemed beyond defeat right now. Occasionally she caught the sound of distant helicopter rotors as the two choppers kept up a search by spotlight in areas farther away from the wreck. The frigid dark made a continued search dangerous for people on foot, but the choppers kept up their valiant duty.

They had long since passed the limit of how far the girls could have walked, so now they were in the territory of a possible body dump. Or an out-and-out kidnapping, although no one seemed willing to say the word out loud.

In fact, no one seemed willing to consider the possibility that it might be too late for the three women. No one. A whole lot of determined people had spent a very long, very cold day hunting in the brush and gullies.

Just as the coffeepot blew a loud burst of steam to announce that it had finished, she heard a sharp rap on her door. Sighing, she rose and went to answer it, trying not to hope it was good news about the missing women. Good news, however, would have crackled over her radio or come by phone.

She opened the door, half expecting to see one of her neighbors with questions about the day's search. Instead she found Al Carstairs. His cheeks were still reddened from the cold, and he was carrying two big brown bags with handles and a tray of tall coffee cups. "Don't know about you, Kelly, but I'm starved and I don't feel like cooking. Care to join me for dinner?"

She couldn't possibly have refused the offer. Not only was it kind, but she really didn't want to be alone with her thoughts. Weary or not, she smiled. "Come in. I just made coffee, though." She reached to help with the cardboard tray.

"I bet it isn't a latte."

Despite all, she laughed. "It sure isn't."

Once inside he carried the bags to the kitchen counter. Small as this house was, the living area and kitchen were a single room, divided by a small bar. Bugle evidently had taken a liking to Al, because as soon as his arms were empty, the dog nudged his leg, then sat expectantly with his tail sweeping the wood floor and displacing a colorful rag rug.

Al obligingly squatted and gave the dog a good scratch around his ruff. Then he straightened and smiled at Kelly. "Bugle's a great dog. Anyway, dinner. I hope you like steak sandwiches. They're the most filling thing on Maude's menu and after today I think we both need calories."

"A steak sandwich sounds wonderful," she said, meaning it. "As many hours as we were out in the cold, I could probably eat a whole one."

The sandwiches were famous, and their size was always huge. Maude had always catered to hardworking ranchers, and people with more sedentary jobs made use of doggie bags. Kelly usually thought of a steak sandwich as two meals for the price of one.

Not tonight, though. She had a feeling she could polish one off in its entirety.

Al began pulling insulated containers out of the bags. He enumerated as he went. "Steak sandwich, steak sandwich, tossed salad, extra rolls for the extra hungry and another pie. I think Maude hopes that if she stokes us all on sugar we'll find those girls."

"Energy will help," she admitted. "I'm worn out. The cold absolutely drained me today."

He smiled her way. "Probably because we never took a break to warm up."

Bugle's nose reached the countertop, and he sniffed, making a hopeful little whine.

"You already had a huge dinner," Kelly said to him.

"He's apparently got good taste, though." Al's great smile seemed to leaven the entire room.

They decided to eat at the bar right out of the

foam containers. "No dishes tonight," said Al. "We've got another long day coming up."

She agreed, and felt no need to apologize for failing to retrieve any of her limited quantity of plates, bowls and utensils.

She'd known Al for several years, but didn't really know him. It was odd, when she thought about it, but his work in animal control didn't often cross with hers as a deputy.

"You have a kennel out behind your house?" she asked him after she had swallowed the first juicy mouthful of the steak sandwich.

"Oh, yeah. Insulated metal building with twenty cages. More like a barn. I seldom need that much room but occasionally it happens."

"But don't the owners want them back?"

"First I have to identify the owners, and that's not always easy. When dogs slip out, they sometimes lose their collars and all too often they're not microchipped. Then there are the dumped dogs."

"Dumped?" She turned her head to look at him. He held up a finger as he finished chewing and swallowing a mouthful of his sandwich.

"Dumped," he repeated. "God knows why, but some idiots think their dogs are equipped to become self-sustaining. Now, mind you, these are animals that haven't had to hunt for a meal in their lives and are used to human care. Most of them, anyway. Some folks hope a rancher will find the animal and take it in. I hate to tell you how often that turns bad."

She nodded. "Why?"

"I've been called out too often by a rancher who's found a dead dog. He could just bury it, of course, or leave it for the vultures, but most ranchers care about animals more than that. So they call me, hoping I track someone down to tell them what happened to their animal. I wish I could. I wouldn't be polite about it."

"Nor would I," she admitted, feeling sickened by the thought of what those animals must have endured. "What a cruel thing to do!"

"Especially when you consider they could have turned them in at any vet's office if they didn't want to hunt up a shelter. The lucky ones get found and fed while a rancher waits for me to show up. They don't need another dog. Mainly because dozens are getting abandoned."

Kelly urged herself to eat more, and felt her appetite returning. "What do you do with the survivors?"

"Kennel them. The vet, Mike Windwalker, does his best to help get them adopted, but it's not like we're short on dogs around here. Or cats for that matter. But cats are better at looking after themselves, especially if they had some time with an older cat who taught them to hunt. And most of our ranchers and farmers don't exactly mind another barn cat showing up. They're useful."

"But the dogs aren't?"

"Not without a lot of training. Cadel Marcus takes some to train them as K-9s or service animals, but there's a limit to what he can do, too."

"It sounds like a serious problem."

"It is." He polished off his sandwich and some of the salad, then encouraged her to eat more. "Another long day ahead."

She didn't want to think about it. Not until it arrived. Reminding herself that she'd been famished, she focused on savoring her dinner.

At any other time, she realized she would have been feeling content. A pleasant, handsome man dining with her, and excellent dinner, Bugle pretending to sleep near the foot of her stool but alert for any falling crumbs.

"That fireplace work?" he asked.

"I believe so. I haven't given it much of a workout because I'm gone too often."

"Wanna try it?"

She shrugged as she was about to put the last bit of sandwich in her mouth. "Sure. It worked fine the one time I used it."

Shortly after she'd taken the job here, having moved from Laramie County. It had been a big change for her in terms of a smaller department serving fewer people overall, but that's what she wanted. Community policing. She'd certainly found it here, and after five years had no desire to move on.

There were dry logs stacked in a box near the fireplace, and he laid them on the grate with some twisted newspaper beneath them. They'd probably light good and fast as long as they'd been sitting there. Then he reached in to open the flue and an empty bird's nest fell out onto the stack of wood.

"I hope that's the only one," he remarked.

"So do I." She'd never had that chimney cleaned and if it was packed with stuff like that, it'd become an interesting evening.

Grabbing a poker, he shoved it up inside the chimney and didn't even loosen any creosote.

"Well, here goes," he said, pulling a butane lighter out of his pocket and holding it to the paper. "If the flame and smoke don't head straight up, I'll put it out."

"Okay." She couldn't even work up any worry about it. Instead she began to gather up the remains of their dinner and put them away in the fridge. Except for the pie. That would be fine on the counter and she had a strong feeling both of them would want a piece before the evening was over.

She looked over and saw the flames were

standing straight up and that no smoke was escaping. "I guess it's okay."

"Right as rain." He remained squatting for a few more minutes while she finally settled into her recliner. There was a gooseneck chair on the other side of the battered side table. Oh, it was apparent that she entertained a whole lot. Yup.

Mainly one girlfriend at a time.

Al straightened, brushing his hands on his jeans. "I guess I should go. I've imposed…"

"You haven't imposed at all," she interrupted swiftly. "Get comfortable. There's still that pot of coffee and…" She trailed off.

"You don't want to be thinking about those girls tonight."

"Not if I can avoid it," she admitted.

"Me neither."

The lattes were long gone so he hunted up two mugs from her cupboards and brought a couple of cups of coffee to set on the end table. "You want anything in yours?"

"Black is fine," she answered. "Thanks."

A silence followed after he settled into the gooseneck chair. She knew why. They were both thinking about the same thing and neither of them wanted to talk about it. Even distractions hardly worked. Three young women were residing at the corners of her mind and wouldn't go away. The second night.

They could be looking only for bad things now.

THREE TEENS HUDDLED beneath a ragged blanket in a dank basement that even during the day had barely let in a crack of light. A pile of protein bars had been dumped in with them along with a bunch of plastic bottles of water.

Their winter outerwear was gone, as were their shoes and phones. In trembling voices, they'd talked about finding a way to escape, but knew in the dangerous weather outside they wouldn't get very far in their thin clothes and bare feet.

All they could do was huddle together beneath a smelly blanket and wait. They tried to buck each other up, but young though they were they knew no good could come from this.

Over the last twenty-four hours, hopelessness had begun to settle in. Tears had been frequent, terror had been constant, and at one point Mary Lou had even suggested they stop using the blanket and huddling and just freeze to death.

The other two girls had gotten upset with her. Chantal pointed out tearily that they had hope only if they stayed alive.

They grew quiet for long spells, feeling wearier and wearier. No protein bar could stave off the fatigue of constant fear.

They sat in the dark, as close as they could get, while their nerves crawled, their bodies ached and their minds ran rampant with horrible ideas.

They had no idea how they'd gotten here, nor

any idea of who had put them here, but they knew there was no good reason for it. None.

EVEN COFFEE COULDN'T keep Kelly from dozing briefly in her easy chair. Sounds drew her out of an unpleasant nightmare and she saw Al putting another log on the fire.

When he turned around, he saw that her eyes were open, and he gave her a half smile. "Want me to leave so you can get to bed?"

She shook her head. She wasn't a coward by nature but this event had disturbed her more than many. "I'm still feeling guilty."

"For what? I saw your report. No damage to the car, no occupants, no reason to think anything except a passerby picked them up to get them out of the cold. It was too dark to look for tire skid marks. I mean…"

She nodded. "I know all that rationally, Al. It's the irrational part of me that's having trouble."

He pulled the gooseneck chair over until he was close enough to offer her his hand. She couldn't help but reach over and take it.

Bugle, finding this something entirely new in his experience, came over to investigate as if he weren't certain anyone should be touching Kelly.

"It's okay, Bugle. Relax."

The dog sniffed their joined hands, then settled on the floor between them.

Al grinned. "He's still feeling protective, I see."

"Always. My buddy." But her mind wasn't on Bugle, and she needed to distract herself or she'd get no rest this awful night, but she had to be bright and ready for the morning. A quiet sigh escaped her.

"Where are you from?" Al asked. "Someone said you used to be with the Laramie police, but I'm sure that wasn't your entire life."

She summoned a smile. "No. Hardly. I've moved around. My dad is Puerto Rican and I was born there. My mom worked as an executive for one of the companies that had a business there, but she died five years ago. Cancer."

"I'm sorry."

"So am I, but given what she went through in the end, her death was a relief." She shook her head a little. She didn't want to go down this road. "Anyway, they moved to Florida when my mom was transferred. My dad was a police officer and he took a local job."

"So you followed in his footsteps?"

"So it seems. I can't remember ever wanting to do anything else, but I essentially won the lottery when I was tapped to be a K-9 officer. I love dogs. Dad wanted me to stay in Florida, but I wanted to come up here. I visit him when I can. At least living in Florida, for him, means people don't look at him suspiciously."

His brow rose. "Why would they do that?"

"He's Latin, Al. With a bit of Indio in him.

I get cross-eyed looks, as well. A lot of folks still think I'm a foreigner. Many people seem to have a hard time believing Puerto Ricans are US citizens."

He was frowning faintly. "I hope you don't run into a whole lot of that around here."

"No more than the indigenous people. Maybe less. I have a badge."

At that he laughed quietly. "That does help."

The smile felt awkward on her face, but it lifted her spirits a bit. She needed that. There wasn't a damn thing she could do right now. She was about to ask him his story when the landline rang.

Forgetting everything, nearly tripping over Bugle in her eagerness, she ran to get the phone. It was Gage Dalton. "I'm sure you're wondering about those guys we questioned."

"Absolutely. Al Carstairs is here. I'm sure he wants to know, too. Speaker?"

"Go ahead. Just don't give me a reverb."

She punched the speaker button, then sat on one of the bar stools. "You're on, Gage."

"Hi, Gage," Al said.

"Howdy. Okay, the long and short of it is that our three interviewees were put off by the way the girls dismissed them. Including our infamous drunk, Art Mason. Judging by what some of the other patrons said, he was in no condition to cross a room, let alone get down a highway.

Jack, the janitor, said they wouldn't let Art leave until he'd drunk a pot of coffee. Way too late for the accident. As for Keeb Dustin, he appeared so appalled by the idea he'd be interested in girls so young that the deputy believed him. Anyway, he only stopped by the table because they were laughing and he liked hearing they were having a good time. Warned 'em to avoid anyone who showed them too much attention, then moved on to the bar, where most folks saw him nursing a few longnecks until after midnight."

"So they're clear," Al said.

"Well, hold on," Gage answered. "At this point I'm not clearing anyone, but yeah, neither seems likely. The place was busy. I'm not sure anyone would have noticed if one of these guys left for a while. Then there's Hal Olsen. Always on the lookout for a pretty woman. Apparently he scored that night because Lydie Dern says he went home with her about eleven or so. In the other direction, so they didn't see anything on the road."

"Dang," said Kelly, who only then realized just how much she'd been hoping they'd get a good clue.

"We'll keep an eye on them, of course," Gage continued. "I've got a couple of men working the tavern tonight, to see if anyone remembers anything unusual about last night, but so far no go. It seems many of them weren't there, and those who were had more important things on their minds."

Kelly chewed her lower lips for a few seconds. "Gage? Were the girls involved in anything that might have drawn attention? What have we got on their backgrounds now?"

"Been working on that. Three young ladies, all with high grades, members of the soccer team and the debate club. If it weren't for the fact that Jane Beauvoir was a member of the chess club, I'd have said the three of them were joined at the hip. Families all attend Good Shepherd Church, no one seems to think they had any enemies, either the teens or their parents…although that can always be a mistaken impression. Enemies don't always announce themselves."

"True. You're saying we don't really have anything."

Gage snorted, audible through the speaker. "I'm saying we haven't found it yet. Abducting three young women from the side of the road before eleven at night is a bold thing to do. It's also stupid, because no matter how smart they think they are, perps always leave something behind. You remember that rule."

Kelly nodded even though she couldn't be seen through the phone. "The perp takes something away but he always leaves something behind."

"We've just got to find it. Anyway, you two

catch up on your sleep. Tomorrow's going to be another long day."

Kelly disconnected and sat staring at the phone as if it might have something else to offer. The ugly truth was that it wouldn't. It was like being inside a dark bag without a ray of light.

Maybe like those girls.

She passed a hand over her eyes as if she wanted to erase her thoughts, then looked over at Al. "It's still early," she said, surprised as her eyes grazed the wall clock. Not even nine yet.

As long as she'd lived up north, some part of her still lived where she'd been born, when night didn't fall so early even in the winter.

"Yeah," he answered. "Not a very helpful call."

"Maybe, maybe not. Weeding things out counts, too. But listen, don't you have animals to look after?"

"Not really. All the pets have been taken home. The rest have enough food to look after themselves tonight. Minks, by the way, don't make friendly pets."

But he was standing and pushing the chair back to its original position.

Crap, Kelly thought. He'd brought her dinner, she'd asked him to stay just a short while ago and now he was apparently taking her question as a dismissal. She slid off the stool, saying, "Al."

He glanced at her. "Yeah?"

"I was asking about the animals, not hinting for you to leave."

"You should get some sleep," he answered. "You heard Gage."

She hesitated, then said, "What makes minks bad pets, and would you like some of that pie you brought?"

He laughed then. "Minks are hard to tame, even if you start when they're still kits. It takes a lot of patience. And that's just the start."

She pulled the aluminum foil off the pie and retrieved two small plates from the cupboard. A knife would have to do for cutting slices. "What's the rest?"

"They prefer a semiaquatic environment, not easy to do at home around here. They can be really aggressive and you can't let them out because they'll kill other minks if any are around, and foxes would love to dine on them. They should be solitary except during mating, and these folks made the mistake of keeping two. They weren't exactly getting along."

"Wow. Worse than ferrets?"

"Depends. They're part of the same family of carnivores, *Mustelidae*. There you've got ferrets, skunks, weasels, even otters. But as long as you get a ferret young and give it plenty to entertain itself, it'll be little trouble. Plus they can be truly affectionate. These minks?" He just shook his head. "Someone will think they're adorable. Someone always does."

"So what will you do with them?" She passed him a slice of peach pie that smelled richly of cinnamon.

He thanked her and slid onto a bar stool.

"Coffee?"

"With this?" he asked. "Absolutely. Maude's pie can make my teeth curl."

That drew a laugh from her. "Lots of sugar. One of the reasons I don't eat them often." She cut herself a slice, then poured coffee for both of them from the waiting pot. It really hadn't been that long ago that she'd made it. This day had been endless.

Well, until now, anyway. She was enjoying Al's company. "The minks," she reminded him.

"Oh, I'm looking for a facility to take them. A zoo, a rescue organization. We'll see, but since they've been fed ground meat by humans since they were tiny, I'm not sure they could make it on their own even if they survived predators."

"Probably not," she agreed, sliding onto the other stool. "I don't know that I'd want to take them on."

"You'd need the facilities to survive it. They're nocturnal but awake a lot in the daytime. They're carnivores. They don't like each other unless they're mating."

"Sounds like some marriages."

For the first time she heard his full-throated belly laugh.

"Well," she said, "it *does*."

"That's what made me laugh. Anyway, I'll find someone to take the minks. As for other animals…we're quiet at the moment. I keep an eye out for strays when the weather's dangerous like this, but most of them go home immediately. No pets have been dumped recently, at least none that have been found and reported to me."

The pie was an amazing combination of tart and sweet. She felt her mouth pucker and revel all at once. Closing her eyes, she gave herself over to the wonderful flavor.

Al fell silent, too, and she could sense he was enjoying the pie as much as she was. It should have felt sinful, with those girls out there in some kind of terrible trouble, but somehow it didn't.

She couldn't spend every minute worrying and thinking about it or she'd soon be no use to anyone. She'd learned a while ago that the toughest part of her job was trying not to get so involved her emotions began to rule her. Separation was essential. Even if she had to go to the ladies' room and cry about it for a while until she could restore her balance.

God knew, she'd seen some awful stuff that still lingered with her.

"Did you grow up here?" she asked, once again seeking a diversionary train of conversation. Although, she admitted, she wanted to know more about Al.

"Yeah, I did. Family's gone now, though. The two of them operated a music store that mostly catered to students who wanted to rent instruments or take additional lessons. I used to love listening to my dad play the oboe. It's such a beautiful, haunting sound, but put him and my mother together on a pair of saxophones and the place would rock."

She smiled. "That sounds wonderful. You musical?"

"Me? Nah. I was at the wrong age to want to do anything my parents did. Bad enough I had to work at the store and sell sheet music and reeds. I used to go nuts sometimes watching a high-school-aged clarinetist try out a bunch of reeds before settling on one he or she liked. No thought to the cost of those discarded reeds, and sometimes I was never certain they could really tell the difference."

Kelly laughed. "I'm sure some could."

"Oh, yeah, but not all of them. I got the feeling it was a thing to do if you played a woodwind. Anyway, my folks didn't mind it, so who was I to get annoyed?"

"What made you leave?"

"Did you know you can die of a broken heart? For real?"

She turned on her stool until she faced him

directly. He seemed preoccupied with reaching for another piece of pie. "Al?"

"It's true," he said, his tone changing, growing a bit sorrowful. "Dad took a road trip to Denver to get some supplies. Unfortunately, he was mugged and killed for fifty dollars and a credit card."

Kelly's breath snagged and her chest tightened, aching for him.

"Anyway," he went on, "Mom died two days later. Broken heart syndrome, they called it. It had a fancier name, of course, since it was discovered by some Japanese doctors, but whatever. Her heart stopped beating right, and she thought the pain was grief and…too late. She was gone."

Kelly instinctively reached out to grip his forearm. "I am so sorry, Al. So, so sorry."

"It was a long time ago." At last he turned his head and gave her a faint smile. His eyes were dry. "Still hurts a bit, but it *was* a long time ago. After I recovered from the shock and two funerals, I put the shop up for sale and went looking for the Marine recruiter. I needed to get out of this town."

She squeezed his arm, then let go. "I can imagine."

He shrugged slightly. "I turned tail, but at the time I was glad I did. Boot camp gave me a whole lot of ways to focus on something else and expend a bunch of anger."

To her it sounded like one rational solution to an overwhelming loss. Somehow she couldn't imagine him trying to run his parents' store after that, and feeling angry every time some-one tossed aside a half-dozen reeds before find-ing the perfect one. He might have let them know what he thought.

That drew a quiet sound of amusement from her.

"What?" he asked, digging into a second piece of the pie.

"I was just imagining you dealing with the stu-dents who tossed aside reeds after all you went through."

That brought the smile back to his face. "It sure wouldn't have been pretty. For a while there I was one angry young man."

"Understandably. I was pretty angry after my mom died, but it wasn't as if there was anything she could have done. She had a particularly ag-gressive form of cancer. Oh, well." Thoughts kept getting dark, probably because of all that had happened in the last twenty-four hours.

Her mind kept wanting to wander out into the icy darkness outside, but she couldn't let it. What was she going to do? Race out into the night and run wildly around?

No, she had to wait for morning, for the brief-ing, for all the details that had been undoubtedly gathered today by various teams. Wait and hope for a major clue.

God, she hated this! She squeezed her eyes closed and battled all the feelings about what those young women might be experiencing, trying to put them away into a box until there was something she could actually act on.

"You care."

Al's voice reached into her dark thoughts and she opened her eyes. "Don't you?" she asked almost truculently.

"Very much. Thing is, being in the military I eventually learned to put things away until I had to deal with them. Once you've made your plans, done your end of it, there's nothing more except to wait for the fallout. If you can't sleep, if you're gnawing holes in your own stomach, it doesn't change a damn thing."

She knew he was right but didn't know how to get to that pinnacle of detachment. It wasn't as if she'd ever had to deal with anything like this in her policing career. "I deal with accidents, robberies, even a rare murder…not abductions, Al. It's different."

"Of course it's different. Worse, maybe, because at this point we can't even be sure those girls were abducted. Maybe they *did* hitch a ride, get dropped off at someplace closer to home and just never made it because of the weather."

She sat up a little straighter. "That's possible."

Then she started crashing again. "There's still the fact that they went off the road without even braking."

"Maybe we'll find out otherwise. Those crime scene techs could pull a needle out of a haystack. Let's wait for the morning briefing. We could well learn something hopeful."

He was right, of course. That didn't change the ugly, dark roiling inside her. Finally she gave up on her pie and covered the pan with the slightly crumpled aluminum foil. "You take this with you when you go," she said. "It's more temptation than I can stand and I need it like poison."

His gaze grew inscrutable. "Okay," he said after a few beats. "Are you going to be okay, Kelly? Seriously? You want me to sleep on your floor? Or you want to come to my place?"

His words made her acutely aware that she wasn't behaving professionally. This was a case, like any other she had worked. It was always tougher when the victims were young, but you had to wade through it. Do the job. Not let it overwhelm you. She was in danger of drowning, not a usual state of affairs for her. She prided herself on being a good cop, not a mess of tangled emotions.

"This is really getting to me," she admitted. "More than things usually do. But I've got to deal, Al. I can't use you as a crutch, no matter how kind your offer is. Call it my learning curve. Especially if I want to stay in law enforcement."

He nodded slowly. "It's learnable. This is just a rough case. Rougher than usual."

She fixed her gaze on him again, turning outward from her inner turmoil. "I can't imagine what you've had to deal with. You were in combat, right?"

"Unfortunately. You make contact once or twice, and you learn how useful a shell can be. You just can't afford to brood about it. The next mess will always come. All you can do is maintain optimal readiness. Consider this your first contact."

"But I've done other things…" She paused. "There was this crash of a light plane. I was among the first responders and…" Again she paused, squeezing her eyes shut. "You've seen it. It was more than a year before I could deal with raw chicken or spaghetti."

"I know."

She opened her eyes. "I've moved past it. Mostly. But you're right. This is so different it might as well be first contact for me. So I just have to push through."

"Take something to help you sleep. Got any melatonin?"

"That stuff is a natural hormone, right?"

"The same thing the body makes. I use it once in a while when memory starts bugging me. Best part of it is I can wake up and one coffee makes me alert again. No hangover."

"I'll keep that in mind." Right then her insides and emotions felt as if they'd been thrown in a blender. But she had to get through it. Tomorrow was another day, and she wanted to be able to help. To be useful in whatever way she was needed. "Thanks, Al. You've been great."

He glanced at the digital clock on her microwave. "I should go. We both need some sleep and I *do* have a few animals I need to check on."

She wanted to keep him longer but knew that clinging wasn't going to fix a damn thing. She needed to find her objectivity and put this case into the realm of other cases, a problem to be solved. There *was* always a possibility this would turn out well. Heck, they might get a call in the middle of the night telling them the girls had turned up at some outlying farmhouse.

As Al was leaving, he paused at the door, pie in hand, then surprised her by wrapping one arm around her and hugging her tightly for a brief few seconds. "You're strong," he said. "You'll make it."

She wished she were as confident.

As she latched the door behind him, it struck her that she was being terribly self-indulgent, giving in to useless feelings and allowing them to run her.

She needed to be thinking, using her brain or

sleeping. Either one would be more useful and less selfish.

When at last she curled up in bed, Bugle stretched alongside her, closer than usual, as if he felt her distress. With her hand digging into his ruff, she closed her eyes and finally, finally fell asleep.

Chapter Five

Once again the sheriff's office was crammed with deputies and city police, and plenty of other people waited outside, wondering where the search would head today.

Because they were going to search. Even as the first, very faint light of dawn began to appear in the east, the helicopters could be heard taking to the air again, to hunt with their spotlights until daylight aided them, cabin crews alert for any movement, or any color outside the norm.

Today they had more information about the missing, however.

"All right," Gage said, rapping on one of the desks for silence. "Micah here is going to fill you in."

Micah Parish, of clear Cherokee ancestry, had been with the office since the days when Gage had first arrived in town. At first he had been greeted with old prejudices, but over the years he had knit himself into the fabric of the community.

"All right," he said, lifting a whiteboard and placing it on an easel. The photographs of the three missing young women stared back at them. "You know these are the young ladies we need to find. We learned something from the parents about what they might be wearing, so keep alert for colors of bright pink, royal blue and, unfortunately, light green. That won't stick out very well. But look for colors that don't belong out there at this time of year."

Murmurs and nods went around the room.

"You'll need to inform the civilians who are searching with us. Given our search area today, we'll have one deputy leading each group of searchers. We can divvy it up before you depart.

"As for other things, the enemies these young women might have…need I tell you that nobody has an enemy?"

A quiet laugh rolled around the room. Dark humor. The kind that kept cops, firefighters and soldiers sane.

Micah nodded in response. "We're going to be talking to some of their friends today, other kids at school. We may learn that there are a few people who actually don't like them, or that they've had a run-in with someone. Kelly?"

She raised her hand so he could find her in the crowd. "Sir?"

"I want you and Connie to do the interviews at school today. The principal is agreeable and will give you a private room. Kelly, I know Bugle is suited to other tasks but his presence may keep the atmosphere more relaxing for the students, okay?"

"Okay, Micah." She could see his point, and much as her body wanted to be outdoors moving, and much as she was sure that Bugle would prefer that, she knew he was probably right. Bugle always drew interested attention.

As THE FINAL bell rang for the day and students started piling out of the high school for buses and their own cars, Connie and Kelly sat back at the table they'd been using in a private room facing laptops and notebooks.

Kelly sighed.

Connie stretched and nearly groaned. "I'm getting too old for this."

Kelly laughed. "You're not that old. Don't make me feel bad."

"You know how I met my husband, Ethan?"

Kelly shook her head. "Before my time."

"Well, he's Micah Parish's son."

That snagged Kelly's interest. She twisted on the folding chair that could have done with a pillow and looked at Connie. "Yeah?"

"Yeah."

"I wondered because of the name but nobody ever told me."

"Well, that was an interesting story. Micah didn't know about him because his mother hadn't told him, so one day Ethan shows up at Micah's ranch with the news. But that wasn't the point of me bringing it up. I brought it up because years ago, when my daughter was about seven, I thought she was kidnapped."

"Oh my God," Kelly breathed.

"Ethan tracked her, believe it or not. We'd had days of this awful tension because a stranger had approached her on her way home from school. Deputies were crawling every street, parents were warned not to let their children walk home alone… The drill. You know it. Then my daughter disappeared during the night out her bedroom window. The thing was, Ethan's background in the military gave him the skills to track her. We found her up at the old mining camp…and the man who had taken her was her father, my ex. He'd just gotten out of prison."

"You must have gone through hell." Kelly couldn't begin to imagine it.

"I did. But it didn't last long and it turned out all right." Connie's mouth compressed, then she said, "It's not looking good, Kelly. Almost forty-eight hours now. The window's closing."

"I know. But it's not immutable." She needed to believe that. She *had* to believe that. Out in the fading afternoon light, dozens, if not hundreds, of people were hunting the countryside, knocking on every door, looking for any sign at all of the three girls. At some point they couldn't keep the search going at this level. Even with all the volunteers, there would come a time when they'd have to give up looking and start hoping for some other kind of clue.

How could three girls just vanish into the night like this?

Because someone had taken them.

She looked at Connie. "We need to start thinking about whether there's anyone around here who might be capable of this abduction."

"We're already thinking about that," Connie reminded her. "We just spent all day asking a bunch of high school students if they'd seen anything odd, if these girls had mentioned being afraid of someone or something, if anyone disliked them enough to want to hurt them. We're already doing it, Kelly."

"It doesn't feel like enough."

"Especially when we haven't learned anything that feels useful. Yet." Connie sighed and closed her laptop. "I need to get home, make dinner for the kids and Ethan, assuming he comes in from the search. I'm going to spend an awful lot of time thinking about what we heard today. You?"

"I'm not going to be able to think about anything else. Maybe somewhere in this shower of love is a needle."

Connie laughed wearily. "Exactly. It was creepy, if you ask me. Kids this age always have some gripes about one another. This sounded like a wake."

No one speaks ill of the dead.

"Yeah, it did. And that bothers me, Connie."

"Why?" Connie's gaze grew sharp.

"Because you'd expect people this young to be convinced these girls were going to show up. Instead they seem to have given up. Why?"

"Maybe because it's so damn cold out there they know no one could survive for long."

"Maybe." But Kelly had trouble believing it. "And maybe I'm overreacting. They're probably all scared about this and just as confused as anyone."

Connie nodded and stood, pulling her uniform parka on. "I'll pass all this non-news along to the sheriff on my way home. The students all have our cards. If they think of something, or suddenly want to open up about anything, they know how to reach us." She smiled wanly. "They'll probably call *you*. Bugle was a hit."

Indeed he had been. He'd even preened a bit, if a dog could preen. Kelly suspected he'd have been happy to stay even longer to enjoy all the pets and praise that had come his way.

But the fun part was over.

"Work," she said.

He needed to hear no more. He stretched and got ready to move. His tail even wagged a bit. He truly enjoyed working.

Which was more than she could say that particular day.

On the way home, she stopped at the diner to pick up dinner. On impulse, she bought enough for two and hoped that Al might be inclined to stop by when the search ended. She told herself it was a silly hope, but she needed something to look forward to, even if she was imagining it.

All this time, Al had never shown any interest in her. Well, occasionally she thought she caught a spark of heat in his gaze, but if so he masked it quickly. Probably she was imagining that, too.

She shook her head at herself as she carried home enough food for an army. No involvement, she reminded herself. She'd seen it happen, when two people in the same department got close, then broke up. The subsequent situation was often uncomfortable for everyone, and sometimes it could grow ugly.

Nope, none of that.

She fed Bugle, who'd lacked only food during the day because she had a special water bottle for him that opened to provide a tray for him to lap out of. No, he'd never go thirsty as long as she could refill that bottle.

He didn't seem especially hungry, however.

He left nearly half his kibble in his bowl, causing her to wonder if she should heat some more chicken livers for him. But no, she didn't want him to expect that every day. It didn't take long for him to create a habit.

A hot shower helped ease some of the tension from her, especially her shoulders and neck, then she dressed in flannel pajamas and a bathrobe, wrapping her hair in a towel. As she emerged into the main part of the little house, she eyed the fireplace. The logs had long since burned out, but she wondered if she should make another fire just for herself.

She certainly needed something cheery after today. On the other hand, burning the wood for her own entertainment seemed wasteful and not especially good for the environment. Last night had been a true splurge but it had been so enjoyable.

The towel damp-dried her short bob quickly, so she went to hang it over a rack and run a bush through her hair. How many kids had they interviewed that day? She'd lost count at some point, although she could check it on her computer or her notepad, where each of them had been dutifully noted by name and age.

It still seemed odd that no one had anything negative to say. She hadn't been in high school for a while, but she easily remembered the cliques and the gossip and the way some of the students had avoided others like the plague.

These three girls were unusual in their pursuits. Not cheerleaders, the perennially popular, but nerds. Chess club? Debate club? Soccer, and not even first string? Either they'd become basically invisible or no one today had wanted to mention the petty kinds of comments students like them often drew.

She bet it was the latter. She'd seen their photos. Nerds or not, they were all pretty enough to attract attention at a hormonally driven age.

Sighing, she fluffed her damp hair a little with her fingers and decided she needed to eat before she took a complete plunge. This entire situation was so upsetting, and she'd never dealt well with the feeling of helplessness. Right now she felt helpless. Closing her eyes, she could all too easily imagine those girls out there somewhere, terrified out of their minds.

Someone had taken them. She believed that now after Al's recognition that the car hadn't braked before going off the road. And for all three of them to have been taken? Drugs.

She felt her heart lift a bit, leaving the worst of her despair behind when there was a rap on the door. She opened it and Al stood there. He spoke before she could even greet him. "I was thinking about picking up dinner for us if I'm not becoming a nuisance. You interested?"

"Already done. Come on in. There's plenty. How'd the search go?"

He was cold enough that when she stood near him she could feel his body sucking the heat from the air. He tossed off his gloves and parka and knelt before her fireplace. "You mind?"

"I was thinking about doing it."

"Then let me. I need it. You know, like a candle in the dark."

She felt her heart and stomach both plummet. "Nothing?"

"Not a damn thing. A glove? A shoe? A scarf? Nope. Not even that much. You?"

"If anyone ever had a mean thing to say about those girls, we didn't hear it today. Tomorrow we'll talk to some teachers, too, but I'm not sure it's going to make any difference."

The dry logs he piled into the fireplace started quickly. He tossed the match onto the flames and remained squatting, holding his hands out toward the fire, lost in thought.

After a few minutes, she asked, "Hungry?"

"Famished," he admitted. A couple of seconds later he stood and came to the bar to help her unload the bags. "You went all out."

"I was seeking comfort," she admitted. And hoping he might stop by, but she didn't want to tell him that.

"You don't have to explain that to me," he agreed. Tonight she brought out dishes. They had a lilac pattern on them, leftovers from her mother's collection that she'd never bothered to add to. A few dinner plates, salad plates and bowls remained. Enough for two people, at a pinch maybe three.

She'd skipped the steak sandwiches and instead had asked Maude for containers of tomato soup and thick grilled cheese sandwiches. More comfort food.

"Ah, man," Al said, "I love Maude's grilled cheese. It's like eating Texas toast covered in melted Havarti. She seasons them, too. I hope you like dill."

"Love it. That's one of the reasons I decided to try them."

"It's a hit and I haven't taken my first bite."

The soup was rich and surprisingly good, Kelly thought. She wasn't the biggest fan of tomato soup but Maude's might change her mind.

Sitting at the bar with Al, feeling the heat from the fireplace warming her back, it was almost possible to believe everything was normal.

It was not.

She ate quickly, trying not to think about whether the missing students were eating anything tonight, whether they were warm enough, whether they were being terrorized. Later, she told herself, forcibly squashing the thoughts. They could talk about all this mess after they finished eating.

One of her previous partners had scolded her for losing her appetite. "You owe it to the victim to keep yourself in the best functioning shape possible."

But sometimes it was hard. Sometimes her whole body and mind wanted to rebel at the idea that anything, *anything*, could be normal in a situation like this.

Al kept the conversation general and light. She gave him credit for that because her attempts to respond in the same vein weren't exactly stellar.

She looked at Al. "After Connie and I talk to the teachers tomorrow, I want to go back to Rusty's tavern."

He raised a brow. "Yeah?"

"Everything seems to have started there, doesn't it? And they said they'd make a list of everyone who was there that night."

Al nodded slowly. "I'll go with you, if you don't mind."

Why would she mind? If police work had taught her nothing else, it had taught her that two brains were often better than one.

Settled in her plan, she resumed eating.

CLOSER THAN KELLY would have believed, and yet farther than it seemed possible, two girls awoke in a darkened basement, chilled to the bone despite the ragged blanket that had been tossed over them.

A single movement, and Chantal cried out. "Wire," she said. "Oh, God, wire." Her wrists and ankles were bound and every movement of the thin, bare wire cut at skin. "Mary Lou? Jane?"

"Me, too," answered Jane, her voice thick as if she'd been crying. "He drugged us again. Chantal, I don't think I can go without water, but it must have been in the water bottles."

"Yeah." Probably. Chantal's mind recoiled, then seemed to stiffen. "Mary Lou? Mary Lou?"

"I don't think she's here," Jane answered, her voice breaking. "She was right beside me earlier. Now she's not answering."

Helplessly, ignoring the cutting pain in her wrists, Chantal edged closer to Jane. "She's gone?"

Jane seemingly didn't even want to answer. After a few seconds she said in a cracked whisper, "Maybe she got knocked out more than we did."

"Shh," whispered Chantal. "Hold your breath and listen."

But there was no other sound in the dank space, not so much as soft breaths. A tomb couldn't have been any more silent.

Mary Lou was gone. But to where and for what?

"Oh my God," Jane whispered. "Oh my God. What did we do, Chantal?"

"That's not going to help," Chantal whispered fiercely. "We've got to get our heads working again. There's got to be something we can do *now*." She *had* to believe that. Never once in her life had she simply given up, even when a situation looked hard. Like trying out for the soccer team. She didn't have any real athletic ability, but she'd wanted to do it anyway because it was the kind of activity that was good for college applications. So she'd practiced until she'd become good enough to make the second string. Because she refused to be defeated by her own mind.

She believed in her ability to conquer the difficult, and she was trying to believe she could conquer this, as well.

But the wire around her wrists and ankles gave lie to that. Hopelessness, as cold and dank as the dark room, settled over her.

REVE HAD HAD ENOUGH. Maybe taking the three girls had seemed like a good idea at the time, but the one he'd just dealt with... No fun at all.

Well, he'd have no more to do with her. He still had two more and if he was careful, they'd probably work better. But he was going to keep them tied up in the dark longer, and keep them a whole lot hungrier. By the time he got done, they'd think he was their savior. Yeah.

In the meantime, he needed to ditch this one. Driving down back roads in the dark with his headlights off wasn't a whole lot of fun, but he was wary they might resume the helicopter search. They seemed to have called it off at dusk, though. Giving up, he supposed.

He didn't go far out of town, maybe ten miles. He knew of some wide-open ranchland that hadn't been used in years, and it would provide the perfect place to dump whatshername. Trash. That's all she was now.

He didn't bother to wrap her in anything. The last thing he wanted was for her body to be protected from the elements or scavengers. Nope, she'd come into this world as naked as a jaybird, and she was going out the same way.

The hard ground aided him, leaving behind almost no sign of his passing. When he got far enough from the road, he stopped.

Damn, she'd grown heavy. Or maybe he was just hurting.

Didn't matter. She was knocked out and would stay that way just long enough. With a grunt, he rolled her naked body into a ditch. Cold as this night was, she'd be dead almost before she woke up.

Then he dragged a couple of tumbleweeds over her, checking to make sure the ditch wouldn't let them blow away too easily.

In a week or so, she'd be nothing but bones. As for her clothes…he had a woodstove to burn them. No sign she'd ever been anywhere near his place.

As for the other two…that abandoned, rundown house was perfect, with a solid basement but everything else going to hell. Nobody ever went there. Not even kids looking for a thrill. In a few years there'd be nothing left of the house except the hollowed-out basement.

Turning slowly, he drove away, making sure he didn't leave any deep tracks behind him. He stuck to old tractor ruts, hard as rock in the dry winter. He wouldn't stir up anything noticeable, and once it snowed there'd be absolutely nothing to see.

The winter had aided him, he thought. Traditionally the area didn't get a whole lot of snow and what it did was dry and blew around. The last couple of years had been unusual with heavier snows, but not this year. Here they had reached January with nothing but a few light flurries that hadn't stuck. That wouldn't last, but it had lasted long enough for this job.

Damn, he ached from that kick. He'd have liked to treat her to a bit of a beating, but he was trying not to leave evidence, and even if all they ever found were her bones, assuming the wolves or coyotes didn't drag them away, they'd be able to tell she'd been hurt before dying.

Nope, teen girl freezes to death in January on the high plains of Wyoming. Wouldn't be the first. No clothes meant only that the carrion eaters had pulled them apart and dragged them away. It kind of amused him to think of the hours that would be wasted seeking scraps of cloth.

He realized he was thirsty and decided to go to Rusty's for a beer or two. He went several times a week and no one would notice him, except maybe for Spence and Jeff, if they were there and wanted to play pool. He had a life.

And the life provided cover.

CHANTAL AWOKE SUDDENLY. The jarring movement reminded her of the wire cutting painfully into her wrists and ankles. She drew a long breath, steadying herself, letting the pain wash over her and then away. Beside her, Jane still slept, a quiet snore escaping her. This basement was causing her allergies to act up, uncomfortable for Jane when she couldn't even blow her nose.

But those quiet snores hadn't wakened her. She listened intently but heard only the lonely sound of the wind. If their captor had come and left more food and water, she didn't know. Not that she wanted any of it now.

A headache pounded behind her eyes, either from hunger or from the drug they'd been given…when? She didn't even know how long ago they'd been knocked out and Mary Lou had disappeared.

All of a sudden she understood why people

would find a way to scratch hash marks for days into the walls of their prisons. Except in here she could not be sure what was night and what was day. There was absolutely no way to keep track of time. That could prove maddening, she realized. As maddening as the endless night that swallowed them.

She stared into the unyielding dark and tried to think of something they might be able to do. Some way to put an end to this. She knew well enough that without shoes and jackets they wouldn't make it very far in the Wyoming winter weather. But some other way, because right now escape looked impossible.

Then, out of nowhere, a deep sorrow welled up in her and as if she'd seen it with her own eyes, she felt the truth in her very bones.

Mary Lou was dead.

She had to stifle a cry, to bite her lip until she tasted blood. How could she know? How could it be?

But she knew. And she didn't want Jane to know.

MILES AWAY, Kelly jerked out of a sound sleep. Bugle, who'd been snoring beside her, lifted his head. The small night-light glowed, her protection against jumping out of bed in the dark for an emergency call and barking her shins or tripping. In that light she could see Bugle's focus. He'd become alert, very alert.

She listened, hearing nothing but the night wind and the occasional crackle from the banked fire in the living room.

Then Bugle made a sound she almost never heard from him. It came from deep within him, a low groan, not a growl, and it sounded so incredibly forlorn that it seemed laced with sorrow. But over what? A bad dream?

Then he put his head on her belly and whimpered softly.

Knowledge crashed in on her. She knew what had wakened her so unexpectedly and what Bugle was trying to tell her. She knew why she felt her chest squeezing as if it wanted to silence her heart.

One of the girls was dead.

Chapter Six

Day 4

His phone rang well before dawn. Al was used to it. He had no set hours and folks knew they could call him if their animal escaped in this dangerous weather. He didn't mind at all. Saving animals was one way he could make up for a bunch of things he'd done that he never wanted to remember. Besides, he generally believed that animals were kinder than people. Certainly more forgiving.

He threw back the comforter, slapped his stockinged feet on the rough would floor and leaned forward to grab the receiver for the landline. "Animal Control. Carstairs."

"She's dead."

He recognized Kelly's voice instantly. "Who is? What happened?"

"I don't know. I just know one of the girls is dead. Bugle feels it, too. Damn it, Al, I'm going to smash something!"

He'd worked with animals too long not to respect their intuition. Plus, Bugle had a link to those girls after smelling their garments.

"Hell, I'll be right over."

"I'm not crazy!"

"I don't think you are. I'm on my way. Give me a few. I need to make sure everyone's got some water."

"Okay." Her voice cracked. "Okay."

He dressed as swiftly as he could, wishing he had more zippers and fewer buttons, then ran out to the kennels in the insulated barn. Two felines and one canine raised their heads curiously but didn't seem at all disturbed. The minxes were snarling at each other from cages five feet apart.

Yeah, they had water. Plenty of food in their automatic feeders. The dog yawned at him and went back to sleep. The cats merely stared enigmatically. The minks ignored him.

Sure that his charges would be all right for a while, he headed out to his truck. The light from the lamp he'd left on in his cabin silhouetted a squirrel in the window.

"Hey, Regis," he said. "What are you doing out at this hour?"

He'd never get an answer. All he knew was that squirrels tended to stay in their dreys at night with the rest of their squirrel families.

Crap, was the whole world suddenly going nuts? A million questions demanded answers but he refused to ask them until he got to Kelly's place. All he needed to know for now was that she was clearly distraught and probably didn't want to call anyone from her department. He supposed he ought to feel complimented that she didn't think he'd dismiss her or label her nuts.

Still, the only evidence a feeling? Hers or the dog's? Yeah, he wouldn't want to explain that to most people, although he wasn't the sort to dismiss it.

He'd been in situations in Afghanistan where feelings of that kind had been all that saved his life and the lives of his squad. The sense that something was about to happen. That someone lurked and was ready to kill.

Easy to dismiss by telling yourself you'd picked up on some small thing in the environment that you hadn't consciously noticed.

This was going to be different.

At three in the morning there was no hope of finding any ready-made coffee unless he drove to the far end of town to the truck stop. That would take too long. Dang, he needed some caffeine as quickly as possible, but he was sure he could make it at Kelly's house even if he'd have to wait fifteen or twenty minutes. She'd probably need some, too, before this night was over.

The drive seemed endless, which it didn't usually, but eventually he reached her little house on the edge of town and pulled into the driveway, two strips of concrete that were wheel-distance apart. An old-fashioned driveway, the kind that had come about in the days of wheeled carriages and wagons.

No getting stuck in mud. Or snow. Or... He shut the stupid line of thought down. The lights were on in Kelly's small cottage. Another time they might have looked welcoming.

The instant he reached her door, the icy night wind whipping through narrowed streets like a hungry animal, she flung it open. She'd been worried over the last few days, but now she looked sunken, circles around her eyes. Bugle didn't even rise from the floor to acknowledge him but lay there looking as depressed as a dog could look.

She couldn't even speak his name, simply stepped back to give him entrance.

"Coffee?" he asked, deciding to start on safe ground.

"I didn't... My hands were shaking..."

This was not at all the competent deputy he'd come to know over the last few years. Not that he knew her very well. They hadn't become fast friends, just acquaintances. But he knew her well enough to realize she was in a place she'd never gone before, at least not in her job. That was saying something because he had a good idea of some of the things she'd seen and dealt with. Law enforcement was the pointy end of the stick in a lot of ways, first responders like firefighters and EMTs. Nightmares that clung.

"Sit if you can," he said quietly. "Get a blanket. I'll start the coffee and build up the fire again. You look like an icicle."

Indeed she did. If he hadn't known better, he'd have thought she'd been standing out in the cold for the last hour.

She needed warmth, maybe food, something to help with the shock.

"I'm not crazy," she said, standing her ground.

"I don't think you are. But let's take care of your immediate physical needs…and frankly mine…before we talk."

At last she settled into her armchair. Bugle unfolded himself and came to place his head on her thigh. Since she'd ignored his other suggestion, Al grabbed the afghan off the back of the chair and tossed it over her, careful not to cover Bugle's head. Kelly's hand dug into the dog's neck as if she were hanging on for dear life.

Her coffeemaker was about the same as his, so stacking it and starting it came automatically, with one difference. He made this coffee strong. Then he nosed into her refrigerator and found a frozen raspberry Danish on a plastic tray. He popped that into the microwave for a quick thaw. Sugar was a good antidote to shock.

It didn't seem like something she'd ordinarily eat, however. But then, what did he know? She had friends who probably came over on week-ends. Most people did. Even him, the isolation-ist misanthrope. Sort of.

At last he got a mug of coffee into her hands, watching them shake a bit, but not enough to spill it. "Want a piece of Danish?"

"Not yet," she murmured.

There was an embroidered stool stuck in one corner, maybe for use as an ottoman. He had no idea, but he had use for it now. He pulled it over until he sat right in front of her with his own coffee.

"Feel any better?"

She gave an almost invisible nod of her head.

"Ready to talk?"

She chewed her lower lip until he feared that she might make it bleed. "I can't explain."

"Then don't," he said gently. "Just give me the facts of what happened. You don't need to ex-plain them to me."

Long seconds passed before she tried to speak again. "It's nuts."

"Don't dismiss it. Just tell me."

She squeezed her eyes closed. "I was sound asleep. I woke up suddenly and it was like…like this tidal wave of despair, maybe anguish…it just filled me. And then I noticed Bugle had come to full alert and he made this groan… Oh, God, I hope I never hear him make that sound again. It was heartrending. Then he put his head on me and he whimpered."

She drew a long, shaky breath. "That's when I knew. Thought I knew. Hell, I don't know. I was absolutely certain that one of those girls had just died."

"I guess Bugle was, too."

She opened her eyes and looked down at her dog. Her real partner. "Yeah," she whispered. "He felt something."

Al rose, then returned with two small plates, each holding a piece of Danish and a fork. "Use your fingers if you want." He set it on her lap and Bugle sniffed at it but left it alone. A well-trained animal.

"The thing is," Kelly said, her voice still thin and a bit cracked, "I can't go to work with this. I can't even tell Gage. He might believe me, but what good would it do? We've still got to look for those missing women."

"I agree."

"I also don't need half the department whispering that I'm losing my marbles if someone overhears me. But damn," she said, her voice nearly a cry, "what can I do? I've got to do something. What if he's going to kill again? Or what if I imagined all this? The stress since the disappearance…"

He reached out and covered her hand with his.

Even as she used her fingers to try to hold on to the plate he'd practically forced on her, he could feel her tremors. And the ice that seemed to be running through her veins.

"Eat. Drink your coffee. You're half the way into shock."

"From a feeling?" She looked utterly dubious.

"From a feeling. That's all it takes sometimes." He knew that intimately from his time at war. Shock could occur from an unexpected emotional blow. She'd had one, regardless of what it was based on.

She managed to swallow half the coffee. He went to get her another cup while she picked at the Danish.

"I don't know what to do." She was gathering her strength again. He could hear it in her voice.

"I'm not sure you *can* do anything," he answered, hoping he sounded reassuring.

"I hope it's not true. I hope I just imagined it because I've been so worried."

"We can hope," he agreed. He was glad to see her drink more coffee and eat a larger piece of Danish. He swallowed his own drink and felt his stomach burn in response. She wasn't the only one who was upset. Usually his stomach was cast iron.

"I must have imagined it," she said a little while later.

"Is Bugle into imagining things?" he asked.

Her head jerked a little as she looked at him. "He might have been responding to me. To my feeling."

"It's possible. I'm going to tell you a story, if you're up to it."

"Why wouldn't I be up to it?"

"Because it doesn't have a happy ending. You're not the first or only person to get feelings like this. They aren't always accurate, but when they are..."

She hesitated, nibbled another piece of Danish. "This was for church on Sunday," she said absently. Then, "Okay, tell me your story."

"Long time ago, a couple of kids I was in high school with went on a family camping trip. The oldest two were avid kayakers. They loved white water. Anyway, the daughter was helping her mother cook dinner when she suddenly looked at her mom and said, 'If I don't go home tonight, I'll never go home.'"

Kelly drew a sharp breath.

"Mom talked her into a better mood, my friend seemed to forget all about it...but the next day she and her brother went kayaking together, they overturned and both of them were lost. So what do you make of what she said to her mom?"

"I know I wouldn't want to live with it," Kelly said, her entire face drooping. "Oh, God, that's awful."

He nodded. "I couldn't agree more. But it's

not the first time I've heard a story like that. So maybe I'm less skeptical than most. I've sure heard some stories about people who knew that someone in their family had died before they got the news. It happens. I can't explain it, but I don't dismiss it. However, in light of the fact that we have no concrete evidence, it won't hurt us to go on hoping your feeling was wrong."

"No, but right now that feels awfully hard."

"I'm sure." It felt hard to him, too. What if one of those missing girls had died? Why? What was the abductor trying to accomplish? To satisfy some ugly need to inflict pain and death? Why three girls, anyway? Seemed like that would make everything more complicated. One you could handle. Three all at once? Difficult.

"I'm sorry," she said unexpectedly.

"For what?" He couldn't imagine.

"For waking you in the middle of the night over something like this. I just couldn't stand to be alone, and I knew if I called one of my friends from the department they might wonder if I'd lost it."

"I don't mind. I'm glad you called, actually." He offered a smile. "And as you can see, I don't think you've lost it." He rose again, stretching muscles that somehow hadn't quite made the transition from bed to being upright, and went to get himself some more coffee. "I get called in the middle of the night often enough. People get worried when their pets go missing in weather like this. I don't mind."

He had settled again on the ottoman in front of her before she spoke again. "So you're a one-man animal rescue team?"

"Sometimes. Mostly the animals haven't gone that far and by the time I show up they're looking to be warm again. Easy enough to find. Although there was one black Lab who didn't give a damn how cold or wet it was. To him, playing keep-away was a big game. I'll never forget that huge grin he'd give me as he pranced out of reach."

She was smiling faintly, a good sign.

"That dog developed quite a reputation in his neighborhood. Jasper. Lots of folks recognized him and got a kick out of him."

"I can imagine."

"You never ran into him? I'm sure he was here during your time."

"Never had the pleasure."

He wondered how circumscribed her life was. Maybe nearly as bad as his own? Nose-to-the-grindstone serious? Of course, he was sure she wasn't the only person in the area who'd never gotten to know Jasper. For most people, if they'd seen that dog he'd have been nothing but a black streak passing by.

The fire was burning behind him, just a small one, but a cheerful sound. However, it was the only cheerful thing in this room. He could feel the cold, as if it had seeped in from the night outside, but it wasn't that kind of cold.

It was the inky coldness of death. There had been times when it had been his nearly constant companion. Now this.

God, he hoped she was mistaken, that the chill he felt had merely arisen from her description of her experience, but he feared it had not. If one of those girls had died, it hadn't been an accident. It had been murder. All that did was make him worry even more about the other two, and worry had already been doing a damn good job of peaking the longer they remained missing.

She'd utterly lost interest in the Danish and coffee he'd given her, so he took them to the kitchen.

"Rest if you can," he told her. "Morning will come soon enough."

He moved the stool back and took the chair near hers, watching her as she stared into the fire, kneading Bugle's neck, her expression both dark and fearful.

At last, however, her eyelids drooped and sleep found her. As soon as it did, Bugle burrowed in a little closer and closed his eyes.

Dog and man kept watch through the silent, terrifying hours of darkness.

A little while later, she stirred and spoke drowsily. "You were in the military, right?"

"Marines."

"How'd you get here, Al? Just because you grew up here?"

But he didn't think that was the story she wanted the answer to. She wanted something more intimate. Deeper. Not superficial answers. Clearly she needed something from him, but what? He couldn't imagine, so he hesitated, maybe too long because she withdrew her question.

"None of my business," she said without opening her eyes. "Sorry."

"No need. I was just wondering how to answer. The facts are simple. I was wounded. Considered unfit for duty. Medically retired. Nothing all that great there. Me and thousands of other troops."

"Yeah." She sighed, and her eyes fluttered open a bit to look at him. "Sad."

"It's the risk you take when you sign up," he said flatly. So true. Except who in the hell really knew what they were signing up for? That was the great secret until you were in the middle of it.

"Anyway, after a while I realized I wasn't dealing well with people. Too angry. Like a firecracker with a short fuse. Animals… Well, they're a whole different story. Being around them is soothing. Uncomplicated for the most part."

"Even minks?"

That drew a quiet laugh from him. "They're

predictable, anyway. With time my fuse is getting longer. I guess I'm finally coming home."

He'd never phrased it that way before, but he could see from her expression that had struck her. She ought to be sleeping but here she was pondering his past and his overwhelmingly philosophical statements. Oorah. Good job, Al.

Chapter Seven

Day 6

Reluctantly, the world resumed its normal course. The search was beginning to taper off. People needed to get back to regular work. The sheriff couldn't afford to keep such a huge manhunt going, and after five days it had become obvious that wherever the girls were, they needed more detective work than traipsing across the countryside.

The families were beside themselves, of course. From the next room, Kelly could hear the sheriff explaining that all they were doing now was shifting focus.

"We'll still be looking but we're not going to find them out in the open," he explained. "We've covered every inch of more than a thousand square miles with our helicopters and quite a bit of the ground on foot. Everybody's been helping and everybody's on high alert for any sign of your daughters. Those girls have either left the county or are indoors somewhere."

"So what do we do now?" Kate Beauvoir demanded. "We can't give up!"

"I didn't say we're giving up," Gage said patiently. Kindly. "We're shifting focus to other methods that we believe will be more useful. The girls clearly didn't run away across open ground. They weren't left out there. So now we concentrate our efforts at a different level. Someone took them and we need to get some clues as to who."

Then the conference room door closed, and the conversation became private. Still haunted by her dream or premonition from two nights before, Kelly was grateful not to hear any more.

The office was too small to offer each deputy his or her own desk, so they shared them, using them as necessary when they were on shift or just coming off and needing to tidy up paperwork. Kelly's share of a desk sat near a window looking out at the courthouse square. The computer that filled a large part of it was an older model, serviceable but needing replacement. A small tray pulled out on one side to provide extra writing space as needed. Creating a sort of wall behind her were three overstuffed filing cabinets. Insofar as possible, records were being retired and placed on microfiche in the basement of the courthouse, but there was still enough paper to jam every drawer.

She had a list of names in front of her, names gleaned from Rusty and his staff, and a few other people who had come forward. The names of those who had been seen at the tavern the night the young women disappeared.

Going through them, she tried to design the most efficient route for herself. Today, she and Bugle were going to knock on doors and ask questions. It was always possible that someone had seen something that might have been suspicious.

Yeah, this was the next level of detective work. Shoe leather.

She heard a door open and instinctively looked up to see the families of the girls leaving. The women all had puffy, red eyes. The men weren't looking much better. Not a one of them seemed happy about the changes.

She couldn't really blame them, she thought as she dragged her eyes down to the paper in front of her. Of course they wanted everyone out there looking. The problem with that was at this point the returns were seriously diminishing. It was a virtual certainty that none of those girls was lying out in the open. Nor had the choppers picked up any sign of disturbed ground.

That meant they were inside somewhere or they were in another county, and Gage had already flashed alerts to every agency within a thousand or more miles. Those girls' photos were going to be burned into the minds of every law enforcement officer in three or more states. Two FBI agents were on their way in from the nearest field office, not that they'd be much help.

Hadn't the mention of the FBI helped the parents a little? Kelly simply couldn't put herself in their shoes. She had no idea how they were assessing all of this, whether FBI agents seemed like they would help.

Even the FBI needed evidence.

Rapping her pen tip on the paper in front of her, Kelly studied it while she listened to the front door close behind the agonized parents. God, she wished she had something to offer them. That anyone here could offer them hope.

But right now hope was fading, and even the parents must realize that. Too long. Too damn long. Even a ransom note would have provided a thread to cling to. But not even that.

Which meant the abductor was up to absolutely no good. None. And that was a whole new level of terrifying.

Much as she tried not to imagine things, she still suffered from the same imagination as everyone else. She'd read enough stories about what had been done to young women who'd been kidnapped and held, sometimes for years on end.

Right now those news stories seemed very close emotionally, very personal.

She pulled out her satellite phone and used the GPS to enter all the addresses she wanted to visit today. Sometimes this county seemed empty, but when you looked at going door-to-door, it grew huge.

When she'd entered the last address, she scanned the map and made the best judgments she could for which order to visit the outlying ranches. The likelihood that anyone had seen anything out there was slender, but on the other hand, those were people who, if they *had* noticed something unusual, would have paid attention. In town, too many people passed through because of the state highway. Roads out by the ranches were an entirely different story.

Satisfied she'd done the best she could, she folded the list and put it in her inside pocket. Then she buttoned up for the cold day and picked up her tablet. Bugle was already moving impatiently. He'd been wanting to get on the road for hours.

Even after all this time and five years here, not to mention Laramie, the first step out the door into the frigid air always felt as if it stole her breath. Once upon a time, as a pup, Bugle had been fascinated by the clouds of steam that came out of his nostrils, but he'd long since learned to ignore it.

As she buttoned him into his caged backseat and climbed into the car that held not one bit of the warmth she had filled it with on her way over, she wondered what Al was doing.

Patrolling? Rounding up escapees in answer to calls? Someday, when she had the time, she thought she might like to go on a ride with him and see what exactly filled his days. It probably wasn't much different from what she did on a lot of days: patrolling in case she was needed. Answering calls that came in if she was nearby. Often the job wasn't exciting. Boring, even. Then there were the other times.

Domestic disputes were the ones she hated most, and they were reaching the time of winter when they ramped up in both number and savagery. Cabin fever, she often thought, was lousy for relationships.

Not knowing what she'd find when she drove onto each ranch and knocked at the door put her on heightened alert. Most people would be friendly, some would even want her to come in for coffee and cookies because they were so glad to see a fresh face.

Her anxiety eased a bit and she smiled through the windshield at a day that was sacrificing all its clouds in favor of bright sun. At this latitude the sun didn't get that high, not like Miami or Puerto Rico, but once the snow covered the ground it would be every bit as blinding.

Right now it was just turning into a beautiful day. She felt a twinge of guilt for even noticing.

She was a little over five miles out of town, driving slowly over a dirt road that was bad now and would be even worse come spring. Thank God it was frozen, but it was like riding on a rubbery roller coaster. To the west the mountains rose like dark sentinels, promising a safety she had never managed to feel. They were close here, and seemed to loom over the county below. The mountains to the east were farther away, beautiful but not quite as dominating. Or threatening. Odd thought.

Just then Bugle started barking his strange half howl, and he persisted demandingly until she pulled to the side on a grassy turnout and put the SUV in Park. "What the heck, Bugle?"

As if he could answer. She could see nothing at all in any direction but dried grasses, scrub and tumbleweed. Oh, and the nearby mountains that right now felt as if they were pressing on her shoulder, leaning in.

He hurried to the left side of the truck and pressed his nose to the window, still howling his fool head off.

She wasn't stupid enough to ignore it when her dog acted like a fool. Something had gripped his attention.

"Okay," she said. She reached for the gloves

on the seat beside her and pulled them on, leaving the car to run to keep it warm.

One thing for sure, she was leashing that dog. If he wanted to chase a rabbit, *she* wasn't going to chase him. He waited impatiently while she opened the door and hooked the long leather lead to the ring on his collar. Then, without so much as a command, he jumped down and began to pull her back the way they had just come. To the point where he'd begun to lose his calm.

Well-trained K-9 or not, Kelly was well aware that he was still a dog. Before she let him pull her completely away from the vehicle, she grabbed a tennis ball, his favorite toy, and shoved it in her pocket. She might need it to get his attention, the way he was behaving.

But he'd raised his head, as if pulling something out of the air. She waited while he sniffed and then blew to clear his nose for a fresh sniff. Okay, maybe not a rabbit.

Then he lowered his head and began to pull her along the shoulder, weaving a bit as he went. The odor he pursued hadn't settled into a straight line, but neither had it behaved that oddly. An animal carrying something? But what? Or was he tracking a scent from something left beside the road?

If he hadn't been so determined, she might have called him back to her vehicle, but she'd learned to read Bugle well. He was onto something that to him was awfully important. Considering his training, what he believed to be important often turned out to be important to her.

She hadn't realized how long she had driven past the point where he started his frenzied barking. Nearly half a mile. With every step she grew more aware of the icy wind. She couldn't imagine what had gotten into the car, but something obviously had, and he was determined to get to it. With each few steps, he grew more focused. More intent. Her K-9 was on the hunt.

She pulled her snorkel hood closer around her face but didn't zip it into a narrow opening. As a cop she knew how important her range of vision was to her safety. Better to have a frozen nose than be blindsided.

Finally Bugle paused. He lifted his head again, turning it a little this way and that, then dived into the field beside the road. Not far. There wasn't even a turnout here, just some sagging barbed wire. But when he dipped three feet into the runoff ditch beside the road, he stopped and sat. Then he looked at her and pawed at the ground.

She recognized the signals. He'd found his target. But what the hell was his target? Sudden worry made her heart accelerate as if she were running the last lap in the Kentucky Derby. She began to breathe more rapidly, which made her chest ache and her sinuses feel as if they were about to crack from the dryness.

Damn weather. Carefully she approached the spot Bugle sat facing. He reached out one paw, touching nothing, but seeming to point.

She saw a dark heap, small, unimportant. Until she got closer.

A glove. A man's glove. Nothing important. Something like that could have blown out the bed of any pickup truck.

It would have meant nothing at all except for her dog's intense interest in it. Target.

One of the missing girls? But none of them should have a glove like this. So if…

She didn't allow herself to complete the thought. She didn't dare hope, not anymore. Not after the last days. But hopeful or not, she had to treat it as evidence.

"Bugle, guard."

Now that he'd found the object of his fascination, she had absolutely no doubt he'd stay put. Not that she'd have had any doubt anyway. Bugle did his job with all the panache and dutifulness of the cop he was. Maybe better.

She trekked back to her vehicle and pulled out a rubber glove and an evidence bag. The glove had been worn. There'd be DNA evidence inside it if the cold hadn't killed it. It might be important, or it might just be some kind of mistake. Heck, it could be a glove belonging to one of the girls' fathers. Bugle sure wouldn't miss that. Probably nothing, she told herself with each step as her nose grew colder. Probably nothing at all.

But she trusted Bugle's instincts and could not ignore them. She thought about driving back to pick up the dog and glove, then decided against it. She needed to scour the ground with her eyes to see if something else might be there. This was a very isolated part of the county, mostly grazing land, few houses, but someone could have come along this road and dropped something else. Or left a track, not that the ground was lately in any condition to take tracks.

She took the walk more slowly this time, forcing her attention to the shoulder right in front of her. It yielded nothing at all, and the rusting barbed wire appeared untouched. Somebody had some work to do, she thought. She didn't envy anyone who had to replace all that fencing.

Then she reached Bugle, who was still at attention but starting to shiver a bit. So much for a fur coat. As soon as she reached his side, she squatted, snapped on a rubber glove after removing her own insulated one and picked up the ratty old glove to insert in an evidence bag.

As soon as it was secure, she said to Bugle, "Search."

But he sniffed around a small area and seemed to find the exercise pointless. Okay, the glove was it.

Taking his leash in hand again, she joined him in a quick jog back to the vehicle. He seemed glad to jump inside the warmth. For that matter, she was glad, too.

Dang, it was so cold. She wondered how the coyotes managed it, because she knew they were out on their rounds despite the weather. She received the occasional call to check out an injured animal. Personally, she thought self-respecting coyotes ought to join bears in hibernation.

Her fingers barely wanted to hold the marker as she scribbled the important information on the evidence bag: her name, the date and time, the location where the item had been found. Then she sealed it, and no one would be able to open it without leaving evidence of tampering.

So careful. She hoped like hell it would do some kind of good for the missing women.

Just a clue. She'd been repeating the words like a mantra at the back of her mind for days now. Just a clue. She hardly dared to believe this might be it.

THE REST OF the day was devoted to knocking on doors, drinking quick cups of coffee or tea as she talked to the ranchers, their families and their hired hands, if they had any. A pointless waste of hours, she thought as she pulled up to the last house on her list.

The road had taken her the long way around,

but the ranch house itself wasn't that far from the outskirts of town. There just wasn't a direct road to it.

She had to knock twice, and her stiffening hands didn't appreciate it. She had grown so cold with all of this that her nerves burned when jarred. Just one more, then she could drive back in the heated comfort of her car and hunt up a hot drink and meal. Loads of coffee today hadn't done her much good. In fact, no good at all. She'd quit after a single sip because, while she didn't want to offend, she also didn't want to ask to use people's facilities. Her mouth felt as dry as cotton now.

Bugle had it easy, she thought wryly. Every time she let him leap out, he took care of business.

After her third knock, the door opened. A bleary-eyed man of about thirty-five stared back at her and shook his head a little.

"Sorry to bother you, sir, but you're Walt Revell, the current owner?"

"Uh, yeah." He looked at her again. "Is… What happened?"

"We've had three young women missing for nearly a week now and we're trying to find out if anyone might have seen something unusual that might help us out."

"Oh."

God, she thought, was this guy drunk or

drugged? Or had he worked all night? Mussed hair, clothes that needed ironing… Well, according to records he lived alone. He probably wasn't good at looking after himself.

He shook his head. "Heard about that at the tavern. Damn shame. But I didn't see nothing."

She doubted he could see past the end of his nose. "Thanks for your time." She handed him her card. "If you notice anything that seems unusual or out of place, give us a call, please?"

"Uh, sure."

The door closed even before she finished turning away. Guy probably wanted to get back to sleep.

As she walked back to her vehicle, she saw that Bugle had his nose pressed to the glass. He was probably sick of being cooped up and wanted to be let out to play.

"In a bit," she said to him as she climbed back in and turned her truck around to head back out to the road. "Soon, Bugle."

He gave a low groan as if that answer didn't please him at all.

JANE AND CHANTAL hardly twitched a muscle. At some point, they had been drugged again, probably because it was impossible to go indefinitely without water. At least the wire bindings had been replaced with chain. Kinder to the flesh, maybe, but no less miserable or escapable.

They both realized that Mary Lou was gone for good. They just hoped she wasn't dead, although in the darkness and quiet they sometimes whispered about it. Neither of them any longer nurtured much hope that they would survive this. At their age, that was an especially difficult conclusion to reach.

They'd lived relatively sheltered lives in this out-of-the-way county where, yes, bad things happened, but not all the time. Living on a ranch, or living in town, they hadn't feared walking the streets in the evening or even felt it necessary to lock their doors. Companies that wired houses for security would go broke out here except for some of the businesses.

But that didn't mean they were totally insulated. The news got through, either in newspapers or on the evening television. They'd heard or read stories of what could happen to young women who were kidnapped by unscrupulous men. The questions floating around in their heads now were whether they were to be sex slaves or sacrifices. Both possibilities terrified them equally.

But they certainly didn't expect to be let go. That left them only a need to fight to survive. No other motive existed any longer.

They huddled as close together as they could, giving in and sitting up to eat the food bars placed nearby, forced to drink water because their bodies demanded it. Sometimes the water knocked them out. Those were the merciful times.

It had gotten to the point where Jane told Chantal that she hoped one of those bottles would contain a lethal dose of whatever was putting them to sleep.

Chantal wanted to argue with her, but her arguments were growing wearier and weaker. To fall into sleep and never awake again was beginning to appeal to her, too, though she refused to admit it to Jane.

So cold. Under the ratty blanket, pressed close to each other, they still grew miserably chilled. Unfortunately, not chilled enough to never wake up. They ached from confinement, from cold, from the hard floor. They hated the smelly blanket that did little enough of what a blanket was supposed to do.

They pressed icy bare feet together, rubbing them to stimulate circulation. They switched sides trying to warm one half and then the other.

Survival drove them, but they couldn't even explain why. Giving up would have been so much easier.

Nobody would ever find them, Chantal thought. Ever. But even as she grew more dazed with time, she squashed that thought every time it occurred.

"You know this county," she said to Jane, her

voice little more than a cracked whisper from a sore throat.

"Yeah. If we're in Conard County." Jane didn't sound much better.

"It doesn't matter. People around here won't stop looking for us. They won't. You know that."

"Then why aren't they here already?"

Chantal had no answer for that. Instead she said, "They'll come. They must be looking over every inch."

"So? We're buried in a basement."

Chantal couldn't argue with that, so she fell silent. But then Jane said, "You're right. They'll even look in basements."

To that they clung as much as they could.

"Just eat another food bar," Chantal said. "If the bastard shows up when I'm awake, I don't want to be too weak to give him a hard time."

So they choked down the dry bars and risked a few sips of water.

Keeping up some strength seemed to be all they had left.

NOT TOO MANY miles away, Al Carstairs had resumed his usual duties in animal control. Mostly. Like everyone else, he was knocking on doors asking if anyone had noticed anything unusual. Like everyone else he was getting a lot of negative shakes of the head.

How could this guy have been so invisible?

How was it nobody noticed something odd about a guy pulling three girls out of a car and putting them in his? God, they must have been drugged, and as such Raggedy Ann would have seemed more like a human body.

But nobody had noticed?

Well, it was New Year's night, and he guessed a lot of people were either at home nursing hangovers, or sitting in the bars, roadhouses and taverns that dotted this county, enjoying the hair of the dog that bit them. Rusty had said more than once that his tavern had been hopping.

The girls had left early, too. With the next morning being Sunday, most people who went out to enjoy themselves probably hadn't called it an early evening. So it was entirely possible that not one soul had driven by during the time when the car went off the road, and the abductor moved them to his vehicle.

What if someone had stopped? The guy could have said, "My sister and her friends had too much to drink. I need to get them home."

And if the person who had stopped wasn't from these parts, why would the individual mention it to anyone? Why even question it?

Kelly had apparently been the first person to come upon the car once the girls were gone. No one else had reported a car off the road. A dead silence seemed to have filled the county that night.

He cussed, which didn't please the stray black Lab he'd picked up. Molly, her name was, and while she had a loving home now, there was no question she hadn't always enjoyed one. She was the only dog he'd ever known that would cower at a cuss word, even one in passing conversation.

He'd have loved to find out who her first owners had been so he could give them a piece of his mind. But she'd been dumped at Mike Windwalker's clinic by a guy who said he'd found her beside the highway. And the guy didn't even live in these parts.

No help. Not that it mattered now. Molly had a good home; she just liked to run. Usually she'd run for a couple of hours and then show up at her family's door. This time she'd stayed out longer than usual and Al had been advised the family couldn't find her.

Well, she'd wandered farther than usual. Much.

Then there was a raccoon back there who'd gotten herself tangled in some barbed wire while attempting to heist the contents of a trash can. She needed to see the vet as well as get a dose of rabies vaccine. Mike would probably keep the animal for a while to make sure it wasn't already sick. Unfortunately, even though it was the wrong time of year, she appeared to be pregnant.

But while he was usually very focused on the animals he looked after, it was different now.

Now all he could think about was the missing girls. Acid chewed at his stomach lining, his mouth tasted sour and a beer sounded too good to a guy who'd been dry for five years now.

Not that alcohol had ever taken over, but he'd become nervously aware a year or so after he left the service that it could easily become a favored crutch. That he *could* become addicted. So he'd quit on his own. Not another drop. It hadn't been that hard because he'd taken charge of it before it took charge of him.

But right now he seriously wanted a beer.

Those girls. Those poor girls. And Kelly. He knew she was out there continuing the pursuit but doubted she was having any better luck. He kept remembering that nightmare or premonition she'd had that one of them had died.

He couldn't dismiss it, much as he'd have liked to, and now all he wanted was to discharge these animals and find her, to see how she was holding up. Because this whole situation was not only horrifying, it was weird.

It was as if something supernatural had swept them away.

He dropped Molly at home with her family. The Clancy kids were thrilled to have her back. Molly had apparently tired herself out, because she collapsed at their feet and grinned.

Mike Windwalker took the raccoon, handling

her with long leather gloves to avoid a bite, and agreed she needed rabies vaccine.

"Pregnant, huh?" Mike said as he looked her over before popping the angry animal into a cage. "Somebody mess up her clock?"

"I haven't a foggy. I take them the way I find them."

Mike laughed. "Yeah, me, too."

As he drove away into the fading light of early winter night, Al wondered where he could find Kelly. Then he remembered his damn radio. Duh.

"Actually," she answered, "I was just about to hit the truck stop for one of Hasty's burgers. You interested?"

"Save me a seat."

Maude made a good burger, but Hasty fire-grilled them. A whole different level.

For the first time that day, things seemed to be looking up a bit. A burger and fries. He smiled wryly knowing his doc wouldn't like it, but since he was fit as a fiddle except for certain lingering effects of a wound, he refused to worry about it. If a single burger had ever killed anyone, he'd never heard about it.

But riding his shoulder like a shadow was concern for those three girls. He hated to imagine what their families must be going through. Not knowing was bad enough from his end.

Hasty's truck stop was full of grumbling

beasts as usual. Inside the café, truckers were scattered around, most of them eating heartily and drinking lots of coffee. They were allowed now to drive only eleven hours a day, and most trucks had trackers on them. For reasons of speed and ease of driving, that meant most of these guys slept in their cabs by day and drove all night. Unless the weather was bad, in which case they reversed, wanting all the clarity of sight they could get.

Tonight was looking to be a long night before breakfast came.

Kelly was already there, at a table near a window. He liked that. He never felt quite comfortable without an open view. He knew it was a leftover from war, but knowing it didn't make it go away.

He slid into the booth facing her and smiled. "Want a pregnant momma raccoon who got herself tangled in some barbed wire? She was dumpster diving."

Kelly blinked, as if she needed to change her location in the world. "Really? Pregnant?"

"Seems way early in the season. I left her with Mike Windwalker. First on the list, treatment for rabies and antiseptic for scratches. Anyway, how'd your day go?"

"It went nowhere," she said frankly. "I must have stopped at twenty or so houses. Nobody saw anything that aroused their interest. At least not yet. I'm hoping that maybe someone has a memory jog and calls. There was one interesting thing, however."

The waitress came over and took their orders. Lots of coffee, two burgers for him, one for her, and a heap of fries. It was the cold. He always ate more. So, he guessed, did she. "So what was interesting?"

"Bugle. We were a little over five miles out on a ranch road when he started to go bonkers."

Al arched a brow. "Is that like him?"

"Absolutely not. He wanted my attention and he wasn't going to let me ignore him. He howled and barked until I thought I'd go deaf. So I pulled over and let him hunt whatever scent had caught his attention. About a half mile back down the road he found a glove. A ratty man's work glove, and he wouldn't budge. I gave it to the sheriff before I came here."

"That's strange," he said, thinking it over. He knew a lot about dogs. The idea that Bugle might have caught the scent of one of the missing girls didn't escape him. He leaned back to let their dinners be served, then leaned in again, keeping his voice low. "They're going to test it?"

"Damn straight. I don't know if it'll tell us anything at all, but it's worth a try."

"Definitely." He lifted his burger, his mouth already watering. "You know how amazing dogs are, Kelly. You don't need me to tell you that if

he caught a whiff of one of those girls he'd recognize it even after all this time."

"I know," she said quietly, almost sadly. "I
don't know whether to be hopeful or not. I mean,
it was in the middle of nowhere. It could have
blown off the back end of a pickup truck, and
there's no way to know where it would have been
headed. So…"

"You're afraid it might be false hope."

"Yeah." She stared down at her burger, then
picked it up with obvious reluctance. "I guess
it's better than nothing. What if we can identify
the DNA? Some guy with a record. That'd be a
fantastic clue."

"But you're afraid it won't be."

She raised her gaze. "I somehow think I don't
need to tell you about the tightrope between hope
and despair."

"No," he admitted. "Come on, eat. Your eyes
are so sunken right now they might fall out of
the back of your head."

That at least brought a smile to her face.

"Bugle out in your truck?"

"Yeah." She motioned toward the window.
"See him?"

He did. The SUV was obviously running to
judge by the steam coming off the hood as a
gentle swirl of snowflakes fell.

"I'm going to get him a couple of burgers,

too," she remarked. "Please don't go sanctimonious on me about a proper diet for him."

At that she drew a laugh from him. "I'm sitting here eating two burgers myself. I'm going to get sanctimonious?"

Her smile widened. "He likes a few fries, too."

"Then let's save him some. I'm betting he's salivating out there, smelling everything that's cooking in here."

At that she finally laughed. "The aromas that pour out all the vents and ducts in this place call to human stomachs and noses for miles. Why should he be different?"

The rest of the meal passed amiably, and apparently the waitress knew the drill when it came to Bugle, because along with their separate checks came a couple of cardboard containers holding burgers and even a few fries.

"No ketchup," said the waitress. "I know he loves it, but you'll never convince me it's good for his stomach."

"I don't want to find out," Kelly agreed as she put a twenty on the table. Plus another five she tucked in the waitress's apron. "You didn't see that happen."

Al laughed and followed suit. They were halfway out the door when his radio began to squawk.

"Carstairs," he answered as they descended the steps into the parking lot. Bugle, in the wise way of all canines, was already standing at the window, his tail wagging like a flag in gale-force winds. He knew a treat was on the way.

Al listened, standing still, while Kelly opened the back door of her truck and put the burgers and fries in for Bugle. The cardboard went into the nearby trash can while the paper wrappers remained with the dog. He knew to lick them, not to eat them.

"I'll be right there," Al said. His voice had lost all cheer. He signed off and shoved the phone onto its belt holster.

"What's going on?" Kelly asked him, disturbed by his change in tone.

"A neighborhood problem dog just burrowed under a fence and menaced a four-year-old girl. Gotta go."

"Can I follow?"

"Sure, I might need you to help me legally confiscate the animal. Bugle could be a help, too."

"Where are we heading?"

"Downy Lane. Four-oh-nine."

Kelly radioed dispatch as she followed Al's van down the road. Velma, on duty again, cracked a laugh. "I heard the call. Bet Al needs you and Bugle more than himself."

"Now, Velma…"

Velma laughed again. "He's good with animals. This one is not a good animal. There's a difference. Only reason that dog ain't gone is pure neighborliness."

The listed address wasn't that far away from the truck stop, maybe eight blocks on the far side of the railroad tracks that rarely saw any traffic these days.

It was a shame, Kelly often thought, that railroads had been replaced by trucks. However, given the mountains around here, maybe the trains couldn't be loaded as heavily as the trucks without becoming unsafe. What did she know?

The house in question was old but well cared for, a late-nineteenth-century structure built in the old "shotgun" style. With a narrow lot, every room added on had been added to the rear. The term came from the saying that you could walk in the front door and hit everybody in the house with one blast of a shotgun.

She was glad times had changed in that respect.

She pulled up against the shoulder—no curbs in this part of town—and waited while Al approached the house. Bugle had wolfed down his treats and was now noisily licking his chops.

The front door opened and a man's silhouette appeared. He was clearly upset and waving his arms. Instinctively, Kelly climbed out, leashed Bugle and approached, standing far enough back that she wouldn't seem like a threat.

"—don't know," the guy was saying, his voice

raised. "Do I have to put bars and special locks on every door and window to make my daughter safe? She's *four*! I thought she was in bed. It's basically early, though, and I guess she got tired of watching TV or saw the snowflakes... I dunno. But she went out in her own backyard—a fenced backyard I might add—and suddenly I heard her shrieking and that beast from next door growling and damn, I never came so close to shooting an animal in my life!"

"Was the dog on your property?"

"You better believe it. Not two feet from her, crouched with his teeth bared. I've had it. That damn dog has threatened people before. Especially her. This isn't the first time I've called you, if you remember. It's time to listen."

Al nodded. "I'm sorry, Mr. Jakes. I think we're past issuing warnings now. Is the dog still out back?"

"I don't know. Fences won't hold him. He could be anywhere by now. But just tell me, Al, who the devil buys a dog to keep it outside all the time? I don't think that hellhound has been indoors once since they got him. Doesn't matter. What *does* matter is that my child ought to be able to play safely in her own backyard!"

To a point, Kelly thought as she listened. There were snakes, raccoons, foxes...but she let the thought go. She could understand Mr. Jakes's fury. Whether the dog would attack the child was irrelevant. What mattered was that no child should have to be threatened in his or her own backyard by a dog that should be properly confined.

"I agree," Al replied, keeping his voice calm. "Is your daughter safely inside now? No one else outside?"

"We're all inside, feeling like prisoners in our own house. Something has to be done about that animal or its owners. At this point I don't care which."

"All right. You all wait inside while we hunt for Cujo. That's his name, right?"

"Like some kind of prediction. Yeah. You got help? Because you're going to need it."

"Deputy Noveno and her K-9 will be helping. If we need more help, I can get it. Just relax indoors while we take care of this."

Still grumbling, Jakes went back inside, slamming the door for emphasis. Kelly really couldn't blame him. Apparently this Cujo had been a problem before.

Al came around to the back of his van and Kelly moved in close with Bugle. "Okay," Al said, opening one of the doors. "Time for long leather gloves. I'm going to give you a muzzle to carry in case we need it." Then he turned and faced her, and he didn't look at all happy. "While I don't advocate it, shoot if you think it's necessary."

Kelly looked down at Bugle. "I think a certain set of teeth will work better."

"I hope so. But I don't want Bugle to get messed up either. I don't know what this dog is capable of. Not yet. I know we've had complaints that he's killed pet rabbits and a couple of cats, but there was no proof to pin it on Cujo. So the owners have been slapped with warnings and some fines for not keeping him properly leashed. Here we go again."

They started by walking through a latched gate into the backyard of the Jakeses' house. It was obvious where the dog had dug his way under a wooden privacy fence.

"I wish the neighbors would put in some wire fencing about two feet down," Al remarked. "Most dogs won't dig that deep."

"What breed are we talking about here?"

"Rottie. Usually good dogs, but there are some…"

"There are always some," she agreed as they walked around the side of the house. She didn't know if it was lack of training or poor treatment. Or, if like some people, some dogs just weren't nice pets. They probably had all kinds of personalities.

The backyard proved to be a nice size for such a narrow lot. A metal swing set stood to one side, and what appeared to be a covered sandbox filled a corner. Large and small plastic balls were scattered about, along with a ragged stuffed doll. Al bent for the doll. "I guess Cujo had him some fun after all." He passed the doll to Kelly, who looked it over. The head had unmistakable teeth marks on it.

Bugle sniffed it and gave one quiet woof. He knew. Kelly just hoped the miscreant dog hadn't torn it from the little girl's hands. That would have utterly terrified her.

Al scanned the backyard, then walked up to the house and grabbed a shovel. He jammed it into the hole under the fence in such a way as to make it difficult for the dog to crawl under.

"Next door, now."

Kelly scanned one more time, looking and watching Bugle, but Bugle didn't seem to be much interested in the backyard after one sniff at the torn doll and a pass by the hole under the fence. Instead, he seemed more interested in pulling her back the way they'd come.

He'd be the best one to have a good idea of where Cujo was hanging out.

"You want Bugle to lead the way?" she asked Al as they passed through the gate in the other direction.

He eyed her over his shoulder. "Like I haven't done this before."

She flushed, grateful the darkness hid it. "I only meant he'll be able to smell the other dog."

"It hasn't rained shampoo recently," Al said wryly. "We'll *all* be able to smell Cujo."

He had a point there. Dogs weren't exactly odorless, even when dry.

The house next door was nearly a carbon copy of the Jakes place. Lights gleamed from the window, so someone should be there. Once again, Kelly stood back near the sidewalk. She knew that her presence might cause trouble if whoever answered the door felt belligerent. Best to let Al handle it. He knew these people.

Belligerence was definitely waiting for him. Before Al could say a word, the man who answered was on a tear.

"Bet that damn sissy Jakes called you. Look, a dog's a dog, and they do things like dig under fences. They get out and run. I don't give a damn. That man has been after Cujo since he was a pup! He just wants me to get rid of him!"

Kelly felt Bugle growing tense beside her, ready to spring into action if need be. She made no effort to calm him down. The way that guy was gesticulating, things could get ugly at the drop of a hat.

"Mr. Hays…"

But Hays didn't wait for Al to speak another word. "My dog ain't doing a damn thing but being a dog. Like anyone else's dog. If that sissy next door didn't have a bunch of cats, he'd understand better. He needs some schooling and I might just give it to him."

"Mr. Hays, are you threatening…"

"I ain't threatening nobody. I just want him to leave my damn dog alone."

At that moment the ill-famed Cujo decided to come running around the corner of the house. He didn't go sit placidly beside his master. No, he bared his teeth and growled at Al. Worse, his hackles were raised. That dog was ready to fight.

Kelly tensed but didn't want to intervene unnecessarily. This was Al's job and he probably knew a whole lot more about how to handle this.

"Call your dog off, Hays," Al said. His voice held the sharp edge of command, a voice that said he was used to being obeyed.

"Why? He ain't hurtin' you and *you're* the one trespassing. I'd be within my rights to sic him on you."

Not exactly, Kelly thought, but bit her lip. *Stay out of it.*

"Mr. Hays," Al said, his voice suddenly as cold and hard as steel, "either control your dog and get him to settle or I'll deem him dangerous and put him out of everyone's misery. Are you hearing me?"

Al, still wearing the elbow-length leather gloves he'd put on, reached to his hip and for the first time Kelly noted he was carrying a collapsible baton on his belt. He pulled it off. That baton could put human or dog out of commission without killing either. With a pointed snap, Al extended it.

Bugle sidled forward, as if he wanted to take action, but the gentlest tug on his leash caused him to settle quietly beside Kelly.

Something must have gotten through to Hays, because he snapped, "Cujo! Here!"

The dog, still snarling, obeyed, standing beside his master, facing Al.

"Leash him," Al said in the same steely voice.

Cussing a blue streak, Hays obeyed. Kelly was grateful to see that Cujo's leash was a chain. She figured he could chew his way through leather in no time at all.

"Now," said Al, "we're going to talk. Unless you want me to take Cujo tonight."

Some kind of sullen mumble emerged from Hays.

"You have been repeatedly warned about failing to keep your dog under control. He is to be leashed any time he's outside your front door unless confined by a fence. Your fence out back isn't doing a damn bit of good to judge by the way he tunnels into the Jakeses' yard."

"He's just a dang dog…"

"A dang dog with a mouthful of teeth and a bite powerful enough to break bone. And the Jakes have a four-year-old daughter who has as much right to play safely in her backyard as Cujo has to be in his…as long as he stays in his own yard. Is that clear?"

"They oughta watch her…"

"And you ought to watch your dog. Quit arguing or I'll get really angry. I'm only halfway there."

For halfway to angry, Kelly thought Al seemed remarkably calm. Although his voice still sounded like honed steel.

"Now, listen carefully because I'm through repeating myself. Cujo crawled under the fence and menaced a little girl…"

"He don't menace nobody!"

"He was just menacing *me* and I'm not four. What's more I've got Deputy Noveno as a witness. Clear?"

Finally Hays stopped arguing and just nodded.

"If Cujo had so much as scratched that little girl, I'd be taking him to have him put down right now. This is not a joke. Are you hearing me?"

Hays nodded glumly.

"Unfortunately," Al continued, "a lot of people want rotties because they're tough and dangerous. But the most dangerous dog is one that's thoroughly trained. You hear me? Ask the K-9 officer there if you don't believe me. Regardless, I'll give you two choices. The first is give the dog up to me tonight. The second is, tomorrow morning take him to Cadel Marcus to be trained. If Cadel can train him, you'll have a dog that won't give you any heartburn but will still protect your family. But if you can't do that…"

Finally Hays spoke. "Heard that Marcus guy is good."

"The best. But Cujo needs to be trained, not running wild. And I don't just mean that he sits and stays. There's a lot more to a well-trained dog than that. So those are your choices. In the meantime, you get a citation for animal at large, and you owe the little Jakes girl a new doll."

Hays cussed again, but didn't argue.

Al pulled his summons book from his jacket pocket, tugged off one leather glove, which he tucked under his arm, and began writing. "Okay," he said as he ripped the summons off the pad and handed it to Hays. "You know the drill. Pay the fine by the date listed and you don't have to go to court. But I'll give you one more warning."

"Yeah?"

"Yeah. If Cadel tells me you haven't left Cujo for him to train by ten tomorrow morning, I'll take the dog. No more chances, Mr. Hays. Not one. The life of a four-year-old girl is still worth more than a rottweiler. Clear?"

A couple of minutes later, as they were about to get into their vehicles to leave, Al came to stand beside Kelly. "I hate to put a dog down," he muttered. "I hope that jackass pays attention this time."

Kelly understood. "I wouldn't want to either, but that little girl…"

"Exactly. Listen, if you don't have other plans, want to come to my place? I know it's a ways out."

She smiled, her heart lifting a bit. How did he do that to her? "My place if you'll be comfortable. I've got an early call."

"Your place it is. Want me to grab some coffee from Maude's on my way over?"

"That would be super."

Chapter Eight

Day 17

Chantal and Jane had passed the point of caring much anymore. The cold was gripping them constantly, and their bodies demanded that they eat. They gobbled down food bars without a thought for what might be in them, and when a big package of sandwich cookies showed up, those disappeared in record time.

They'd even stopped worrying about what was in the water bottles. Survival had come down to instincts they could no longer ignore. With chains holding them, they huddled close and were even grateful when a second blanket appeared with the food while they were sleeping. Sleeping or knocked out. They didn't know.

They felt they were being watched sometimes, but were past caring about that, too. They struggled to get the second blanket wrapped around them with the first. It, too, stank, but it smelled like an unwashed body.

"He never met a washing machine he liked," Chantal said, a weak attempt at humor. She couldn't see Jane at all, but heard what sounded like the breath of a laugh.

They'd stopped asking why. They couldn't imagine why they were captive, and they'd given up hope that Mary Lou wasn't already dead.

Chantal, though she'd never said so to Jane, remembered that moment when she'd felt as if Mary Lou had said goodbye. If she was dead, at least she was out of this. Safe. Free of the cold and the terror.

The food warmed them temporarily, as did the extra blanket, and this time when she started to fall asleep, Chantal thought it was natural sleep.

At least she hoped it was.

WALT REVELL, Reve to his friends, came back from a pool game and a few beers at Rusty's Tavern and pulled off the road. It was dark, the moon dropping behind the Western mountains, but there was still enough light to see by. Grabbing a backpack out of the rear of his truck, he began the trek to the collapsing cabin where he was keeping his girls.

Day by day he could see he was winning them over. They talked less, they ate without trying to avoid the food or water. They'd become his creatures, without will of their own.

Not much longer now. He just had to decide

which one seemed most ready to behave herself. He wasn't going to ask much, after all. Some cooking, some cleaning, a little sack time… Not much at all in exchange for continuing to live.

Oh, yeah. No talking. He'd hit 'em into next week if they gave him any lip.

He counseled himself to patience. He'd been too quick with the first one, thinking terror alone would control her. It had been a waste, but he still had two left. He just had to wait until they forgot how to hope.

And from what he could see, hope was beginning to desert them.

When he was sure the drug in the water had done its work, he unlocked the metal door and descended the steps into the basement. He dropped more food and water beside them, a roll of paper towels to let them know that if they behaved they might get more comforts from him.

He hesitated over the cookies, then decided it was too soon to give them yet another reward. Let them eat the dry food bars and drink the water.

When he kicked them lightly with his foot, they barely stirred. Just a few more days. Not much longer.

Already the cops were near to giving up. The female deputy who'd shown up at his door hadn't been especially inquisitive. He could feel her dismissing him mentally. He was a nobody. She probably thought he was stupid.

Good thing she'd left her dog in the car, though. He was scared of what a dog might smell.

Terrified if he were to be honest. Maybe it was time to suffer through another shower and throw some of his clothes in the rickety machine.

Smells could give him away. He didn't want to risk that, not when he was so close to achieving all he wanted.

OVER TWO WEEKS had passed since the girls had gone missing. A feeling of despair was beginning to settle throughout the entire department. Kelly felt it when she went into the office nearly every day. The girls, they had begun to believe, had been taken far away from here. How else could there be no trace of them or their abductor?

Kelly supposed that at this point they'd give anything for a ransom note, but it was getting too late for that. Way too late. For all anyone knew, the girls were already being moved underground by some trafficking outfit, long since out of the county and maybe out of the country.

Kelly couldn't bear to think of it. Nobody wanted to say it out loud, but she was sure they all feared the same thing. The girls' families were at the end of their rope. The FBI agents who had promised to show up were acting on the idea that the women were no longer in the county and thus they were operating out of Denver.

They might be right, but it scalded everyone in the Conard Country Sheriff's Department to feel that the FBI considered them to be too useless to even talk to.

Each day as each shift set out, every single deputy was determined to find something that would help locate the girls. Despairing or not, they certainly hadn't given up. They all feared that some pervert had them in his clutches and was treating them like slaves and whores.

When they could, the helicopters took to the air for an overflight, but had found nothing. Everything out there on the open expanses of wintry range looked as it always had.

And they still didn't have the DNA analysis back from the glove yet but were expecting it hourly. If it would answer any questions, no one knew.

Kelly started visiting Rusty's Tavern on the weekends. Al joined her. A beer, a chance to watch everyone without being obvious. Bugle resented being left at home, but Kelly didn't want to take her departmental SUV. It would be like walking in in full uniform, and her personal vehicle didn't have accommodations for leaving Bugle for long periods. All she wanted to do was watch, anyway.

As if, as Kelly had told Al at one point, the

kidnapper was going to be wearing a sign around his neck.

Leaving no stone unturned had begun to take on a new meaning. Martha knew why they came. She didn't mention it, but she once said in passing, "I'm paying attention."

Kelly believed her. If one person did anything suspicious, they'd be facing Martha, who looked perfectly capable of breaking a beer bottle and using it as a weapon.

Rusty greeted them with a nod, as if to say he was keeping an eye out, as well.

After two weekends, Kelly and Al were both beginning to recognize the regulars. Some of them Kelly had questioned in the days immediately following the abductions, like that Revell guy. Watching him play pool, she wondered if he'd ever learned to color inside the lines.

A silly, useless thought, but a couple of other guys at the bar seemed to like to play with him and bet him a dollar at a time. Nobody was going broke or getting wealthy.

Al talked her into line dancing the second night they were there. All of a sudden her body felt awkward, as if parts wouldn't move right.

"Just relax," he said. "Nobody's watching, everybody's too busy watching their friends."

He was probably right, but she'd never felt comfortable dancing. He slipped his arm around her waist, showed her the simple steps and murmured in her ear, "Treat this as undercover work, a chance to watch people."

Well, that darn near worked like magic. Forgetting about what she was doing, she stumbled only once and Al steadied her. But he was right about watching people. Standing in line with other dancers, facing yet another line, sometimes wheeling around the floor, gave her an excellent chance to take in faces without being obvious about it.

Not that a face was going to tell her anything, but she could hope.

"This is a waste of our time," she said as they returned to their table, the bowl of nuts and two sweaty beer bottles.

"Maybe so. You're the cop. But we're reasonably certain our guy had to find our gals here. Whatever he did, he might try it again." He gestured with this bottle. "See that table over there in the far corner? Take a peek but don't zero in."

She took a quick look and felt her heart slam. Seriously? Two teen girls were sitting over there? They hadn't heard what had happened?

"Indestructible," Al remarked. "At that age, they all believe it."

Won't happen to me. Kelly could almost hear herself saying that from her high school days.

"Anyway," he continued, "unless you have an objection, I figure we'll stay until they leave and maybe follow them at a reasonable distance."

"That's a great idea." She was embarrassed not to have thought of it herself. But then, she'd failed to be observant. That was part of her job. Al had picked up on those girls.

"I must be getting too tired," she remarked. "I should have noticed them."

"Maybe so, but I had a lot of years where I couldn't afford to overlook so much as a misplaced pebble."

That snapped her thoughts to him. "You never talk about it."

"Most of us don't. Nothing like war stories to ruin a mood, ruin friendships or convince folks we're totally crazy."

"I don't think there's any way I could believe you're crazy."

"You haven't seen some of my finer moments." He turned the beer bottle in his hands, and she noticed not for the first time that he seldom drank any of it. He held it like a prop.

"War takes a toll on everyone," he said presently. His voice was pitched so as not to travel. "Some guys come home and put on a veneer that fools everyone. They're okay. Or so everyone thinks, and that makes it easy on the people who care about them. Some can't do that. They need help dealing with what they saw and did. Me, I was somewhere in the middle for a while. Now I'm on the smooth veneer side."

"But is that good for you?"

He shrugged. "Whatever works. I consider myself lucky that I don't have to wallow."

"I doubt I'd think of it as wallowing."

He smiled faintly. "I didn't use that word seriously. I just mean I'm lucky that I don't have to dwell on it all the time. Animals are my medicine. I love the critters."

"Even rotties? By the way, did that dog ever get to Cadel?"

"Cujo is in boot camp right now. And I made sure Cadel knows the situation. Cujo isn't going to get an easy graduation because he doesn't have an easy owner."

That was one way of thinking about it, Kelly decided. The dog was probably going to be more responsible than his owner. That could create an interesting set of problems.

When she thought about Bugle, however, she had some idea of a dog's capabilities absent someone to tell it what to do. "Did I ever tell you about the time that I caught one suspect and Bugle chased down the other?"

"What?" The word came out on a laugh.

"Yup. Pulled a car over. I was getting the data on the registration when the driver climbed out, hands up. So Bugle and I both exited our vehicle. Then for some unknown and unexpected reason, the passenger jumped out and took to his heels. So there I was with the driver at gunpoint and my dog haring off into the woods after the passenger."

Al laughed. "I can just see it."

"Wasn't much to see except his hindquarters and tail. Well, I knew the driver was under the influence but with a backseat full of Bugle's cage, there was no place to put him. Certainly not in the front seat of my vehicle."

"God, no!"

"So I handcuffed the guy and made him run with me as we chased Bugle. Not a happy suspect, I can tell you."

"I imagine not."

"Got lots of body cam footage of him complaining he was tired and could we please take a break. Me, I was worried about getting to Bugle before the other guy could hurt him. For all I knew he had a gun or a knife. Anyway, by the time I'd followed Bugle's bark, and caught up, Bugle had the other guy on his knees with his hands over his head. Never laid a tooth on him."

Now Al was really laughing. "I wish I could have seen that!"

"It *was* quite some scene. And not exactly what I expected. Bugle undertook to make an arrest on his own initiative. Very cool."

"Was it a good arrest?"

"Absolutely. The guy he chased couldn't quite ditch all the cocaine in his pockets before I got there. And there was more in the car. I'm glad to say backup wasn't far behind because at that point we might have been stuck there for a little while, two suspects and no place to put them."

Al smiled. "I love stories like that about animals."

"So you're really crazy about them?"

"Let's just say I think the world would be a better place if we took a few lessons from dogs and cats. They pretty much live in the moment, their spats are never designed to harm one another in any serious way. Think of wolves."

"Wolves?"

"Yeah. They create family groups and take care of each other. Yes, there's a hierarchy, and the omega may have to eat last, but she *will* get enough to eat. And her job is to be the family clown, basically. The social grease that prevents things from growing tense. And as near as anyone can tell, they don't bear grudges."

"We could all do with a few less grudges."

"The girls over there are getting ready to leave," he remarked. Before she could move, he threw some money on the table, then sat back and watched.

Finally he said, "They're out the door. Nobody seems to be watching or paying attention."

"Okay." She rose and he followed suit. Together they eased through the crowd. Kelly bumped into a guy she didn't know. Right behind him was a man that she seemed to recall interviewing. Revell, that was it. This time he looked a little neater and a bit drunk.

"Deputy Kelly," the first guy said heartily. "Going so early?"

"Cut it out," said Revell, looking nervous as if he expected trouble. "Jeez, Spence, not every woman on the planet wants you to take a pass."

Al slipped his arm through hers, his face smiling but a tightness around his eyes. His entire posture seemed to turn into a warning or a threat as he eased her toward the door once again.

It struck her, as they eased their way out toward the door, that their cover was useless. Spence or whatever his name was had made her as law enforcement. So sitting in this damn tavern was probably a waste of time. Hell. Sure, they were trying to make it look like they were dating, but how many believed that?

"Hey," Spence called after them, "you ever find them girls yet?"

At that instant the bar grew immediately silent. Even the live music from the small stage trickled away.

Kelly felt herself stiffening, wanting to turn around and give the idiot a piece of her mind. Those missing girls were no joking matter. Not even for a drunken jerk. Still, she refused to yield to her baser impulse.

"Pretty damn bad," said Spence, "when the

law can't find three girls. Bet they're right under your noses somewhere."

"Let it go," Al said quietly.

Oh, she didn't want to let it go. The anger that had been growing in her in response to weeks of worry wanted to erupt into vesuvian proportions, to flatten the guy's face just for the pleasure of wiping that smirk away.

But Al kept her moving toward the door. "We've got some girls to watch," he murmured.

"Dammit, Spence," she heard Revell say from behind. His tone still sounded a little nervous, but few people wanted to argue with the law. "You tryin' to get yourself in trouble? You're still on probation, remember?"

"So announce it to the world," Spence said angrily. "Just pointing out that cops shouldn't be out havin' a good time when them girls is missing. Get off my case, Reve."

Kelly focused on the door and the girls they were going to keep an eye on. They mattered, not some drunken blowhard who couldn't resist poking at a cop. Almost as if on cue, the band on the stage burst into a rowdy rendition of "Friends in Low Places," singing it about as well as anyone could except the original artist. Which meant poorly.

She drew a steadying breath of icy air as they left the stale beer and noise behind them. Without a word, Al hustled her into her car in the passenger seat. When he held out his hand, she gave him the keys. He hadn't been drinking and frankly, given her response to the idiot back inside, she wasn't at all sure how much she'd put away. Two bottles? She usually had her temper on a tighter tether.

Al wheeled the car around and started down the state highway, following the only visible taillights, the ones that must belong to the young women who'd just left the bar. At least no one else had tried to follow them. Not yet, anyway.

"That Spence guy was right."

"No, he wasn't. He thinks we were there having fun. Far from it, and you don't need me to remind you of that."

"No," she admitted. "But we still should have found *something* about those girls by now."

"This situation stinks," Al announced.

"No kidding."

"You're certainly tied up in knots. I'm getting there."

She twisted in her seat to better see him in the light from the dashboard. "It's not like I can forget those girls. I'm positive my imagination has been doing its worst."

"It has for all of us." He surprised her and reached out, covering one of her hands with his.

She watched the taillights ahead of them, then squeezed her eyes shut briefly. "You know, I've been a cop for nearly ten years now. I'm good at separating the job from the personal. Usually. This time I can't do it, Al! Those girls are haunting my every waking moment. Yeah, I'm still doing my job, but I'd like to be a whole lot busier. Instead I spend a lot of time driving back roads hoping for a glimpse of something useful. Anything. And I keep praying the girls are alive and all right."

For long minutes he didn't speak. The car ahead of them reached the edge of town, turned down a street, then pulled into a driveway. Clearly these young women were getting home safely tonight.

"Job accomplished," he remarked before turning onto another street and heading for her place. "What's getting you wound up," he continued, squeezing her hand, "is that it's been so long and the outcome is not at all promising. You didn't need me to say that, did you?"

No, she hadn't needed to hear it. She felt it in her bones. Since the night she'd wakened from a dead sleep to sense that one of the girls had died, she hadn't been able to believe this would end in any way other than tragically.

"I guess I'm begging for closure," she said after a pause.

"We all are. I can't imagine the hell those parents are living. Our share of it is nothing by comparison."

At that she felt embarrassed. "I'm being selfish."

"I didn't say that. I'd be worried about you if you didn't care this much. We aren't robots, Kelly. We do what we do because we give a damn, you know? There'd be something wrong with you otherwise."

She remembered her dad speaking about a case that had tormented him for years. "Maybe you're right. My dad had some cases that haunted him."

"Let's just hope this one doesn't have to haunt us. There *is* still hope."

But not much, she thought grimly. "The glove didn't tell us much." Their one clue. Basically useless.

"Well, we know it touched one of the girls. Bugle was right about that. But whoever wore it…"

Whoever had worn it wasn't in the database anywhere. So no criminal history, at least not since law enforcement had started to keep such records. "Useless," she said aloud.

"Not if we find the guy. The DNA can tie him to the girls, right?"

"To one of them, at least. Yeah, that could be useful." But only if they found the perp.

She sighed, thinking this was very unlike her. Hope was usually the last thing she tossed overboard when the seas grew choppy. Yet here she was, arguing with every possible strand of hope Al tossed her way.

"I need an attitude adjustment," she said. "Some separation and a tighter focus on solving the crime."

He didn't argue. He turned into her driveway and switched off the engine. "Shall I stay or go?" he asked.

"Stay. Please. Talk me down."

He gave a mirthless laugh. "Maybe you can talk me down, too."

Once again she felt embarrassed. She'd been so busy thinking about how she felt that she hadn't given enough thought to how he must be feeling, as well. The idea that men didn't feel anything…well, her own dad had raised her to realize otherwise. No stoic stiff upper lip for Hector Noveno. He was a man who hadn't been afraid to shed a tear.

As soon as she opened the car door, she knew something was wrong. She could hear Bugle barking, something he rarely did, and he sounded…seriously disturbed.

She hit the ground running, then realized Al had the keys. Had she locked the front door? She didn't think so. She heard the pound of his feet right behind her.

"He doesn't usually do that, does he?"

"No. No." He was upset and communicating it in the only way he could.

She was sure she'd left the front porch light on, but it was off now. Burned-out bulb? Maybe.

Criminy, she'd come out for the evening without most of her usual gear, not even a flashlight. Only her service pistol rode on her belt, hidden by her jacket and a bulky sweater. But the streetlight offered almost enough illumination to see the door and try the knob. If they needed the key they'd probably need the car headlights, as well.

But the knob turned under her hand and she threw the door open only to have Bugle launch himself at her and push her backward.

"Is someone inside?" she asked as she staggered back and regained her footing.

"He doesn't want you in there," Al agreed. "All I've got is my baton."

She lifted her jacket and tucked it back. "I'm armed." Unsnapping her holster, she drew her Glock. "A flashlight could be useful."

But that would take time. She had plenty of them inside, and a couple of good Maglites in her official vehicle, but how long would it take to get them?

"Bugle."

The dog immediately came to her side. "Find."

Well, that didn't get his attention. "Seek," she commanded.

She could have sworn he shook his head but marched forward. Something in the way he moved told her the threat was gone but that something else had seriously bothered him. As soon as they were inside her small foyer, which gave a view of everything on the ground floor except her bedroom, she flipped the overhead light on.

Then she saw what had upset her dog, and wondered how someone had managed to do that without Bugle latching onto him.

A stuffed toy rabbit lay on the floor, and wrapped around its neck was a ragged piece of pink cloth. She didn't want to think about where the cloth had come from. "Time to call for help." Her voice had flattened with tension.

Then she moved slowly back through the house while Al called for reinforcements. She saw the damage before long.

Bugle had been in the bedroom, the door closed. Yeah, she must have done that. He liked to sleep on the bed while she was out, and closing the door was an almost automatic response on her part to dampen winter drafts.

But someone had taken advantage of that, and now her bedroom door had been clawed until Bugle had managed to get free. Long after the miscreant was gone.

Then she set the safety on her gun and sat in her armchair with her hands dangling between her legs, staring at the toy rabbit.

A message? A taunt? A threat? But why?

INSTEAD OF COOKIES, Reve's next reward to the girls was slipper socks. He worked weekends at the hospital as a janitor and had access to plenty of them. He also had access to the drugs he was giving the girls, but nobody would notice such small amounts missing. He didn't need much; it wasn't like he was going to perform surgery.

Anyway, he'd been hearing their complaints about how cold their feet were and it finally dawned on him that neither of them would be very useful or attractive without feet.

He'd seen a gangrenous limb at work once, and he was absolutely positive that he wouldn't want it in his bed. Besides, it would stink.

It was a good thing he'd decided not to let Spence in on his plans because after tonight it was obvious the guy couldn't keep his yap shut. Taunting a cop? That was a good way to get arrested and maybe worse.

The wrong cop, too. People thought Reve was dumb. He kept his head down, didn't say much and often pretended not to hear even when he had. He made himself invisible.

But Spence had drawn attention his way, however indirectly. And that cop Noveno with the dog…she wasn't giving up on the girls. He saw her prowling even when she wasn't on duty, crisscrossing the county like she hoped to spy something.

It might be necessary to get rid of her, he thought as he popped the top on another beer and settled at his own creaky kitchen table. Nearly everyone else seemed convinced those girls were long gone, vanished into some shadowy trafficking organization.

Which, now that he thought about it, might have been a good way to make some money. But no, he wanted those girls for himself. The guys with money could get plenty of girls to enjoy, but Reve…he didn't have the money. He had to find and catch his own or do without.

The catching part had come to him only lately, but after some thought and planning, he'd thought he'd done pretty well. Only one girl lost, and that was because he'd grown too impatient.

He'd learned something and was putting it into practice right now. A few more days, a week maybe, and those girls would be putty, willing to do whatever he said to get out of that basement, to get warm, to eat real food. Yeah. It was working.

But Spence had better just keep his mouth shut. He didn't want that cop's laser gaze trained his way. He swore that Noveno woman had the evil eye or something.

Regardless, if she started hanging around too much, he wouldn't hesitate to eliminate her. See, he wasn't dumb. He knew words like *eliminate*, and that's exactly what would happen to Kelly Noveno if she started hanging around this end of the county too much.

For that matter, Spence, too. He'd better just

stop giving the cops a hard time. No need for that crap. Reve had waited too long to fulfill his dream. He wasn't going to let anyone get in his way, including Spence.

Damn, what had possessed the man, anyway? It was almost as if he was taunting Reve rather than the cop. But Spence didn't know what was going on, so how could he?

Reve rubbed his head, trying to ease a growing headache. Maybe he ought to just stay home for a while, avoid the tavern. Maybe he ought to let the girls be for a couple of days. They had enough water. Didn't matter if they didn't eat for a few days.

Yeah, time to lie low.

Chapter Nine

Day 18

Having the crime scene team crawl all over her house wasn't the most enjoyable experience in the world even though Kelly understood it all. It had to be done. The furry bunny with the odd bow had long since been bagged, but someone had entered her house and perhaps left traces behind them.

She patiently answered questions, but there were no real answers. Al stuck around and explained, too. They were hanging out at the tavern on weekends like a dating couple—two whole weekends, thought Kelly. Some dating—and keeping an eye out for anyone acting strangely.

Which led to the overwhelmingly huge report that they'd watched over several girls, making sure they'd returned home safely. Gigantic effort. Maybe they'd get a medal for valor.

Ah, damn, she thought, letting her head fall back in the recliner. As a cop she was messing up. Her stakeout at the tavern wasn't helping a damn thing. She was too emotionally involved, so much so that a piece of evidence could possibly walk right under her nose without attracting her attention.

And what was with the stuffed rabbit? Somebody's bad idea of a joke?

Gage had dragged himself out of a warm bed to come over here and keep eyes on things. He'd headed up the CSU before he'd been elected sheriff when Nate Tate retired, and he probably knew damn near as much as anyone in this room.

"The rabbit," Gage said, pulling the stool over to sit on.

Kelly came to herself. "Want this chair, Gage? You've got to be miserable on a stool."

"I'm probably less miserable than you are right now. The rabbit."

"Yeah, the rabbit. I have no connection with rabbits, Bugle doesn't especially want to chase them, and…" Suddenly she looked at Al. "There was that guy we spoke to about his rottie. You mentioned the dog had killed some pet rabbits."

Al nodded and shrugged all at once. He was perched on a bar stool. "If Spencer Hays wanted to make a statement about that, my place would make more sense."

"I was with you when you talked to Hays."

"And you stayed well out of it. No, this is something else. Damned if I know what."

Gage bent, wincing as he did so, and picked up the rabbit now safely encased in a clear plastic evidence bag all marked up for the chain of evidence. He stared at it, turning it over a couple of times. "That ragged cloth bothers me. It's impossible to tell if it's supposed to be a bow, or a noose."

Kelly felt her heart skip. "A noose?"

Gage didn't answer her, but instead looked at Al. "How well you know this Spencer Hays? Had many dealings with him?"

"Not many, unless you count the number of times I've had to warn him to keep his dog under control. The dog, by the way, is with Cadel Marcus right now. Time for some decent training before a little girl loses a hand or her face."

Gage nodded thoughtfully. "Well, we'll take a closer look at Mr. Hays. If he thinks you two have been going to the tavern together often, this could be his roundabout way of getting to you, Al. I can't see any other reason to leave it here."

"I've been spending quite a few evenings here," Al said. He didn't offer an explanation, for which Kelly was grateful. He *had* been spending a lot of evenings here when she wasn't working, but she didn't place much importance on it except they were growing a friendship. A very special friendship, she believed, closer than she'd enjoyed in a while. But still just a friendship. How could anyone hope to get at him through her?

After a moment, she decided to bring up the scene at the tavern. "Hays did have something to say to me tonight about not having found the girls yet. He was loud and noisy about it. But I can't imagine when he could have left the rabbit."

"He had time," Al said. "While we followed those girls home. How long do you suppose he needed to dump a stuffed toy here? Was your door locked?"

"No." So maybe he *did* have time. "It still doesn't make sense. It's hardly a threat. A taunt? But why?"

Gage spoke quietly. "Or just to say he knows how to get to you."

Aw, hell, thought Kelly. Aw, hell. "But why?"

The answer to that was a ringing silence.

IT WAS NEARLY one in the morning. Kelly needed to be on duty at seven. She ought to be sleeping but sleep appeared to be far away.

Al examined her bedroom door. "Gotta hand it to Bugle. You're going to need a new door."

"I'm not surprised."

He sat cross-legged on the floor and looked across the room at her. "You're a beautiful woman, Kelly Noveno."

She caught her breath, morose thoughts flying away to be replaced by astonished wonder. "What brought that on?"

He smiled. "I've been thinking it for ages."

She shook her head a little. "You've avoided me for ages. Come off it, Al."

"Sorry, lady. Been avoiding you because I'm a bad bet for a relationship. But that didn't mean I didn't notice. Anyway, sometimes I'd see you and it was like I lost my breath. But…beauty isn't a foundation, and my foundations are shaky anyway."

"You keep saying that. Or versions of that. Just what do you think is wrong with you?"

"If I can't trust myself, why should anyone else trust me?"

He shook his head and stood. "I don't want to leave you here alone tonight."

"I have Bugle," she reminded him.

He nodded slowly. "You're on duty in the morning?"

"Yeah. I hear there's a storm coming so I'll probably be doing welfare checks most of the day." Looking in on older residents who lived out of town, who might need a better place to stay for the duration or who might need some help stocking the larder, in which case she'd give one of the volunteer groups a call.

"Okay, then. I'll see you around."

A moment later he'd disappeared out the door. *See you around?* Had she offended him? All she'd done was ask what he thought was wrong with himself.

Well, if he was going to react that way…

Shaking her head, she climbed into bed wearing her thermal underwear, with Bugle's warmth snuggled up against her beneath the quilt.

A dog was more reliable than a man any day, she thought. She should have figured it out years ago.

But as she drifted into sleep, she had dreams of a rabbit wearing a noose, of a girl in a torn pink jacket, of Bugle with his teeth bared.

Bugle stirred nervously beside her but didn't wake her. His eyes never closed, though.

IT TOOK A hell of a lot of effort. Chantal was past worrying whether she cussed in the silence of her own mind or if she did it out loud so Jane could hear. It didn't seem to bother Jane, anyway.

They were chained so that their hands could reach their mouths, but not much beyond. Her wrists were sore, so sore that she was sure they must be scabbed over. Every movement hurt, but she steeled herself to ignore it. Their ankles were tethered to some kind of ring in the floor, giving them a few feet to move around in, but no more.

Her body felt as if it were crawling in filth. It had been so long since last she'd been able to get clean. Living worse than an animal.

The man hadn't been back in a couple of days, but she was sure he'd return. He wanted something from them and she was certain it was nothing good. They had to find a way to get out of here, except there was no way out except by the stairs that led to the metal door. A storm cellar, she thought. An ancient storm cellar, except over her head was the remains of a window. That seemed odd, so maybe it had been mostly a root cellar.

Whatever it was, it was boarded over with just the slightest cracks that sometimes let in some pale, watery light. Not enough to illuminate the room, but enough to sometimes tell her whether it was night or day.

The nights and days had all run together, though, and she no longer had any idea how long they'd been here.

She just knew she couldn't take it any longer. She was past caring if she died.

She stirred a bit and felt her elbows touch her ribs. For the first time in her life, she could feel her ribs sticking out. To think she'd once wanted to be that thin.

If she ever got out of here alive, she swore she was going to eat herself sick on every kind of junk food she could get her hands on. Her mind played tricks on her now, and sometimes she was sure she could smell a hamburger. Or a French fry. Or even broccoli.

Broccoli? Man, that was desperation. Worse yet, sometimes she craved Brussels sprouts, what her little brother called cannonballs. She'd never liked them, but now she'd have traded a whole lot for a big bowl of something green.

It was dark again, and she could faintly hear a wind whistling. It seemed to be coming from the remains of the window above her head.

"Jane?"

"Yeah." Jane sounded flat, as if she'd totally given up. Chantal was on the edge of it herself, but not quite ready. She had to make at least one attempt, and out of the fog of hunger and darkness an idea had come.

"Can you reach that window above us?"

"You're kidding, right? That's no window, that's jail bars."

"I know, but there are these small cracks in places. You saw them when we talked about them a few days ago." Or whenever it had been. Time had ceased to have meaning.

"So?"

"What if I rip off a piece of my sleeve with my teeth? Do you think you could shove it out a crack?"

"What good will that do?"

"It's bright. If the wind blows it like a flag…"

Jane was silent for a long time. "If it'll make you feel better, I'll try it, but it's a waste of time, Chantal. If it blows away, it says nothing. Anyway, who's going to care about a scrap of cloth? I don't think anyone's been looking for us for ages.

They probably think we're in Mexico or getting whisked away by a gorgeous European prince."

Chantal fell quiet for a while, then said, "Being in a palace sounds better than this."

For the first time in forever, she heard Jane laugh. The noise was cracked, almost broken, but it sounded so good to Chantal.

"I like that," Jane whispered. "A big, rich, handsome prince who'll fall head over heels for both of us and treat us like priceless jewels."

"I think your mom was right when she said you read too many of those books."

Jane snorted. "Better than your cowboy stories. Didn't you ever want to get farther away from here? You don't really want some cowboy to lasso you, do you?"

"Depends. Not the cowboy who has us now."

Once again their mood darkened.

She felt Jane stir beside her. "I can just about reach the bottom crack," she said. "Give me that piece of cloth."

Of course, it wasn't that easy. The way Chantal's teeth felt right now, she wasn't sure they wouldn't all fall out of her head if she tried to tear at something.

"I want a hot shower," she murmured. "I want to be clean again, all over. I want to eat a double cheeseburger."

Jane was silent for what seemed the longest time. "Give me a piece of that cloth," she whispered finally. "If nothing else, it'll be a good grave marker."

Chantal caught her breath. "You think he's leaving us here to die?"

"How should I know? All I know is Mary Lou's been gone forever. If that guy ever wanted anything from us, it was probably before we looked like filthy scarecrows."

Chantal squeezed her eyes shut, holding back tears that couldn't fall anymore. It was as if she had gone dry.

"Come on," Jane said, sounding broken. "The cloth. At least it'll tell them who the skeletons are."

NOW REVE DIDN'T dare do anything about the girls. Not since Spence had opened his yap. He'd have to wait a few days, see if that damn woman cop homed in on Spence in any way.

Talk about skating near the edge. And Spence didn't even know what was going on. It was as if some evil demon had put words in his mouth, causing him to draw attention to the very thing that Reve wanted to keep buried.

Crap.

And that stupid man had actually entered the deputy's house to leave part of an animal skin, he said. To give her a scare, he said.

They'd been lucky her dog hadn't been able to break out of the other room. Reve had spent the whole time sitting in his truck wondering if he should just find a way to shoot Spence when he was out running his trapline.

Another stupid thing. Spence lived in town but thought he was some kind of mountain man. Setting traps for foxes and selling their pelts. Damn fool was lucky he didn't catch himself a bear. Didn't matter. Fox trapping was legal. Wasn't nobody who liked the vermin.

But still. An animal skin?. For the cop when it was the animal control guy he was mad at? So what if the two had started dating. Only a fool went after a man's woman.

Spence was a fool.

Sitting at his kitchen table again, Reve pondered what he was going to do about those girls. He didn't dare go near the place right now, not after the cop had been warned something was going on. What if she drove out here and saw him approaching that tumbledown shack. She might wonder. She might even think he had something to do with that damned toy.

Oh, he'd planned it all so carefully, but he hadn't counted on his friend being an idiot. Hadn't counted that foolish remarks might draw the wrong kind of attention.

Well, he'd better come up with a plan now. The girls had enough food and water for another five or six days. Then there was that storm moving in. If it was as bad as they were predicting, he might not even be able to reach them for a while.

They could die out there.

And right then that didn't sound like such a bad thing to Reve. He'd be shed of the problem and there'd always be another day down the road where he could try this again.

One thing for damn sure: he couldn't do anything from a prison.

Damn Spence all to hell.

THE MORNING BEGAN with an eerie light, a flat grayness that was still quite bright. No shadows fell anywhere, but the breeze, strangely gentled, still whispered of dangers to come.

Al stood outside, making a mental plan for the coming storm. They still had a couple of days, so it was too early to be worrying about wandering animals that might freeze, but he still had his regular tasks. At least they gave him an excuse to roam the county, hoping for a glimpse of something that might tell him what had happened to those girls.

Because he seriously doubted that if they were in this county that they were still alive. Hiding them from neighbors, even out on isolated ranches, would be hard to do for long. People visited, saw each other at church. Only someone who'd been a recluse forever would be overlooked for long.

Kelly had said she was going to be starting her welfare checks. Most of the deputies would be dropping by homes to find out if anyone needed heating oil or supplies, or to come to shelter in town.

So another blanket of searchers was going to be out all day, setting up things to help folks out, but still getting a good look at the entire county. Two days wasn't a long time to set up deliveries of heating oil if very many people were getting low. Impossible to know now, too, how long people might be shut in after the storm. Sometimes the wind blew the snow away like so much dry powder. Other times it built it into huge banks that covered houses until they were nearly invisible.

Only time would tell on that one.

And three girls, if they were out there and weren't being properly cared for, were probably already dead.

The thought darkened his mood considerably as he climbed into his utility vehicle, the one that had been modified to hold four cages comfortably in back. More than four and he'd have to bring them back to shelter.

Today he determined to head outside town, because any lost or abandoned animals were likely to be facing the most trouble out there.

As he bumped along the roads, however, he drifted into thoughts about last night. Spencer had been an ass, for certain, but the man always had been. At least he'd finally seen the light about his dog, Cujo.

But then there was that stuffed rabbit. What in the hell did that mean? That it was a threat was obvious, to him at least. Dismiss it as a toy, but it remained someone had entered Kelly's house without her permission in order to leave it. Not a friendly gesture at all. He made a note to check with her later to ensure she was locking doors and windows. She shouldn't need a reminder but there'd been no evidence of a break-in at her house last night. Someone had opened the door and just walked in.

If he were Kelly, he wouldn't be feeling terribly safe after that. But she hadn't wanted him to stay. Of course, she had Bugle. He was probably more useful than ten armed guards, but still, Al hadn't liked being dismissed in favor of a dog.

But she had Bugle. And he'd had to come home and worry about her.

Then there was that stupid moment when he'd blurted how beautiful she was. Holy cow, what had possessed him? It was like something had taken over his mouth and issued the words before he could stop them.

Then that stuff about how he wasn't good for a relationship. It was true, of course. He hadn't lied about that, but he could see the questions dancing in her dark eyes, and if a guy was going to say things like that, he ought to be willing to answer the questions.

He guessed he spent too much time with dogs and cats. The idea amused him, but it was true. A flick of a tail, a long look, a twitch of ears, those animals could communicate entire encyclopedias to each other.

Him, not so much. He needed to use the whole dictionary of words to make his points. He was out of practice, though. He'd come home from the US Marines, mustered out with a disability, and discovered he had more problems than some shrapnel-torn back muscles. Nope, he had a brain problem, a brain full of rage that could be triggered unexpectedly. He'd gotten better with time, but that monster still lay in wait, and he treated it with wary respect.

What woman needed that? Hell, nobody needed that.

Then, like a great big wheel, his thoughts returned to that damned stuffed rabbit. No mistaking it was a message, but what kind? Why would anyone want to scare Kelly? Yeah, she'd found the car by the roadside, but that had proved to be useless. No information there to explain how three young women could vanish from the planet.

He smiled into the brightening day, with its strange light that assured him the sun was rising somewhere, as he recalled a conversation he'd overheard the other day at Maude's diner. Two men were absolutely convinced the girls had been abducted by aliens.

Vehemently convinced, even to the point of arguing when another fellow had discounted it after overhearing them.

"Where else could they be?" one of the men demanded. "Not in this county, that's for sure. You ever tried to keep anything secret around here?"

Interesting question. If those teens had been taken by someone who lived here, even if he'd transported them out of the state, he'd managed to keep it secret. And the guy at the diner was right. Keeping a secret around here was nigh on impossible.

"Ah, hell," he said to his empty truck. "Just keep your eyes peeled. He had to have left a track somewhere."

Sure. Like he'd left traces they couldn't find in the car. The abduction had been well planned, no question. But to what end? He hoped like mad those girls were still nearby and could be found somehow. That at the very least one of them escaped to seek help.

But with each passing day that hope seemed dimmer.

So did the sky all of a sudden. Though he seldom cared to listen to the radio while he cruised around looking for animals that were out of place, he turned it on now.

Wicked storm on the way. It would hit full force by the day after tomorrow. No searching in the middle of that.

His radio squawked and he picked it up. "Animal control, Carstairs."

"Al," said a familiar voice belonging to an elderly lady outside town, "my Ruffles hasn't come home since yesterday. Not even to eat."

"I'm coming, Mrs. Jackson. Did she seem all right yesterday?"

"She was fine when I let her out yesterday afternoon. Just fine. And she knows how to hide from them coyotes. Heck, I think they're terrified of her."

"Maybe so," he agreed as he used one hand to execute a three-point turn. "I'll be there in fifteen minutes."

She thanked him, her voice wavering as it only could when a person was really upset.

He hoped to God he found Ruffles, an independent, stubborn, single-minded Maine coon that had plenty to say about how life should work.

Yeah, he wouldn't be surprised if that cat scared the coyotes. She was almost as big as some of them, big even for her breed. And while Maine coons were sweet tempered, this one had a temper.

She was also bred to withstand the kind of weather that was coming. Which was about the only good thing Al could say about it.

WHEN HE REACHED Mrs. Jackson's ramshackle ranch about ten miles beyond town, she was standing on the porch bundled up head to foot and calling Ruffles.

This was not good, he thought as he pulled his own jacket on and bundled himself. Ruffles had never run away this long before. A few hours, maybe, but overnight?

As soon as he reached the porch, he urged Mrs. Jackson back inside. She was in her eighties and like many older people she had grown thin and a bit stooped. No meat on her bones to keep her warm, winter-weather wear notwithstanding.

"It's too cold for you to stand out here. You wait inside. You know I always find Ruffles."

"Ruffles has never been gone this long before," she quavered.

He hated to imagine how long she had worried before she finally decided to call him. Several hours at least. "I'll find her," he promised. He just hoped he'd find Ruffles alive and well. "Say, are you set for the storm? Heating oil? Food?"

Mrs. Jackson lived alone, something he couldn't afford to forget.

"I got my heating oil last week," she answered. "I've got food."

"Well, I'll take a look at things in the house once I find the cat," he said. It wouldn't hurt to make sure her heater was operating correctly, and that her idea of food didn't amount to a single can of beans or soup.

She nodded, looking forlorn, and disappeared inside. She continued to peer out the front window, however, pulling the sheers back so she could see.

Okay, Al thought. *Where the devil would you be hiding, Ruffles?*

Something must have scared her good, Al reasoned. More than usual if she'd taken to hiding and didn't want to come out.

He walked around the house, peering at every possible place that cat could have gotten herself stuck. Troubling him, however, was that he didn't hear a single *mew*. If the cat was in trouble, it should be calling for help. They usually did.

A gust of wind caught him, reminding him the weather was about to turn bad and the cat must be found, Maine coon or not.

Sighing, he started to survey the area around the house. A culvert, maybe? But coyotes could get in there. Ruffles didn't seem like the kind of cat that would allow herself to be cornered.

Then he spied a big old cottonwood, bare of leaves for the winter, but still high enough to attract a climber. Giving a mental shrug because he'd never known a cat to get stuck in a tree—

they always seemed to find a way down, usually by jumping—he started to walk that way anyway. He'd made a promise.

As he walked, he scanned the ground almost out of habit. He could read the tracks of animals that had wandered through here before the winter had hardened the earth to cement.

Yeah, lots of coyotes, he saw. A wolf? Maybe, although they usually came in packs. Probably someone's stray dog. Cat tracks, mountain lions. They didn't usually come down out of the mountains this far, but one of them would be big enough to give Ruffles a bad time.

Then he saw a scrap of pink cloth. Just a torn scrap, but a different color from the one from last night's stuffed rabbit. Bending, he looked at it, then scanned the area around. Nothing for over a mile. Still…

First he took a photo with his cell phone, crouching close. Then, touching the scrap only with his glove, he picked it up and tucked it in a seldom-used breast pocket on his jacket. Screw DNA, he guessed, but if he left it here it would blow away. Probably a useless exercise anyway.

Standing again, he continued his trek toward the tree. It was beautiful in the spring and summer, when it was all leafed out. Worthy of photographing. Right now it looked like a bunch of skeletal fingers, something he didn't want to think about.

If that cloth in his pocket had come from one of the missing teens… No way to know. Pink fabric was everywhere, and where could anyone be out here? Mrs. Jackson would know what was in her basement, and she wasn't likely to be involved in a kidnapping.

Still, he'd bring it to the sheriff's attention. Maybe they'd want to look around more out here. In case.

And all the cases were ugly.

"Ruffles." He called for the cat, hoping to see a huge Maine coon come running out of the sagebrush. No such luck. A big tumbleweed came at him, though, brushing by before the wind died again.

It was then he thought he heard a faint sound. "Ruffles?"

Another gust snatched it away and he froze, waiting to hear it again. He needed to locate it, and one sound wasn't enough out here. Sounds, he'd long ago learned since moving here, could be terribly deceptive in the wide-open spaces. Almost as bad as when they echoed among the rocks of mountains.

He resumed his march toward the cottonwood but kept scanning the ground. Where there was one pink piece of cloth, there might be another. There might even be a trail.

Like bread crumbs in Hansel and Gretel, he thought with sour amusement. Yeah, they should be so lucky. Those girls should be that lucky. Damn near three weeks now, and he was holding out very little hope.

He'd had to stop by the Episcopalian church two days ago, a tiny little building, to help the pastor with a barn owl that seemed to be caught in the belfry. While he was there he'd seen Jane's mother lighting a candle. Lighting a candle. It was enough to tear out a man's heart.

But hope endured, somehow. That woman hadn't given up but by now she must be wondering if God was even listening.

He reached the foot of the cottonwood and saw the ground had been ripped up. Coyotes. Then he heard another, faint *mew.*

Looking up, he saw Ruffles, her flecked brown coat blending well with the tree branches. Well, that explained a lot, he thought. Coyotes had treed the cat and she was afraid to come down. Must have been a pack of them or she'd have used her claws and teeth and sent them packing.

"Hey, Ruffles," he said in a soothing tone. "Rescue has arrived. Wanna come down?"

Because he sure didn't want to climb that tree. Winter slumber had probably made a lot of branches brittle, and there didn't look to be many really strong limbs positioned for a man to climb.

But the cat, like most cats, had a problem. She

couldn't back down the tree. Cats just wouldn't do that. They had to see where they were going.

"Come on," he said. "You don't want to be the first cat I've ever seen who couldn't get out of a tree. I bet there's a can of food waiting for you right now. Aren't you cold?"

Talking to a cat. Okay, he was crazy, but at least it was harmless crazy. Anyway, hearing his voice, Ruffles appeared to be relaxing a bit. No coyotes were going to come if the man was here. He just hoped she realized that.

He was also glad this wasn't their first encounter. Ruffles knew him so she had no reason to fear him. He wasn't a stranger. Given the solitude in which Mrs. Jackson lived, there probably weren't a whole lot of people whom Ruffles knew and would trust.

"Come on, sweetie. Did those mean coyotes scare you? I wouldn't have thought they could tree you like this. You prefer life on the ground, don't you?"

Maine coons were definitely not tree cats, preferring to be on the solid earth, but Ruffles must have been terribly scared to perch herself up there.

Not knowing what else to do, he unzipped his jacket and spread his arms invitingly, ignoring the cold and hoping he looked like a safe landing place.

Ruffles looked in every direction, assessing

threats, he assumed. Then her green eyes fixed on him again. Much to his relief, she started to ease her way down. Not easy, headfirst, and she froze often, as if uncertain of her purchase.

Then, in one daring leap, she jumped down on him. He just managed to catch her, feeling her claws trying to dig in through his sweater, and hold her close. Those green eyes stared at him, then a purr told him most of what he needed to know.

Good. He grabbed a flap of his jacket and wrapped it over her. Then he spied some flecks of blood, almost invisible on her mottled coat. Hell, those coyotes had gotten a piece of her.

"I'll get you fixed up," he told her soothingly. "Bet you'd never guess I have a first aid kit for animals in my truck, would you? But I do. Some safe antiseptic. If you get to licking your coat, it won't sicken you. I think of everything, don't I?"

Ruffles's purr grew louder. Happy cat. All was well. For the cat and Mrs. Jackson at least.

RUFFLES HAD SOME scratches and had lost a few tufts of fur but no apparent bite marks, even though he and Mrs. Jackson went over every inch of her. Of course, that thick coat of hers had probably protected her from worse. Once he'd put the antiseptic on her, Al went down into the basement and checked out the heater. Everything appeared to be in working order, and the battery in the carbon monoxide detectors both in the basement and upstairs appeared to be reasonably fresh. He found some new ones in a drawer and changed them out anyway.

Her cupboard wasn't exactly overloaded with food, but she had considerably more than a can of beans. She'd be able to heat food on her propane stove.

Then, as she sat in her rocking chair with a now-happy Ruffles in her lap, he squatted before her.

"The storm is going to get very bad, Mrs. Jackson. No one can say for sure how many days you might be cut off from the world after it passes through. Would you rather I take you and Ruffles to the church shelter?"

She shook her head. "I'm fine. Besides, I was born in this house and if I'm going to die, I'd rather do it here. Been through bad storms before, Al. We'll do all right."

He nodded. "Just call if you need anything. I'll find a way to get here. Promise me?"

"I promise."

He had to be satisfied with that, he supposed. Then he hit the road again, wondering if he should take the scrap of cloth directly to the sheriff or wait until he finished his rounds.

Damned if he knew what use it would be, but maybe he ought to just turn it in. It felt almost as if it were burning a hole in his breast pocket.

So at the end of the driveway, he turned back toward town. The eerie light had changed and become purely leaden.

Winter was about to do her worst.

Chapter Ten

Day 20

"That piece of cloth has been gone for more than a day," Jane remarked wearily. "I told you it wouldn't do any good."

"I think we should try another one."

"You would. Don't you *ever* give up?"

Chantal struggled until she could reach her friend's hand. "What's the point in giving up?" she asked, her voice raspy. "At least we're trying everything we can. Better than just waiting to die."

Which was what they seemed to be doing. As far as they knew, the guy hadn't come back. The water supply was diminishing. The food bars had become a smaller pile. Jane mentioned rationing what they had, but neither of them had the brainpower left to figure out how.

They just resorted to sharing the food bars when they absolutely *had* to eat and taking only small sips from the water bottles.

"You haven't given up either," Chantal said. "If you had you'd finish the water or food."

Jane was silent for what seemed like a long time. "It's night out there," she said finally. Her voice sounded rusty. "Night. You hear the wind? Bad weather."

Indeed Chantal could hear the wind. Whatever cracks this place possessed often whistled from it.

"That's why the cloth blew away."

"Then let's try a piece of my sweater instead of my undershirt. It's thicker. It'll jam in better."

"And unravel."

"God, don't be so down. I can tie off the threads. I'm a knitter, remember? I made this darn sweater."

"At least it's bright green."

"Most visible color in the spectrum," Chantal mumbled, remembering her physics class. "Chartreuse. Okay. It might take me a while, but I'll unravel enough to stick in the crack."

"Better than doing nothing, I suppose."

Yeah, it was, thought Chantal. She was so weary she had to struggle to keep her eyes open, and she couldn't seem to stop shivering. Shivering was a good thing, right?

She twisted, crying out once as her wrists screamed, but she got hold of the bottom of her sweater near the seam. She'd made that seam, she could unmake it.

Then they were going to fly another little flag.

REVE THOUGHT OF the girls in the cellar a mile or so from his house, but with the storm coming and the roads covered with cops doing welfare checks, he decided it would be smart to leave them alone. They'd either make it or they wouldn't.

Since Spence had shot off his fool mouth, though, Reve had been questioning if he'd been wise to abduct those girls so close to home.

He'd had his eye on them for a while, of course. Bright shiny faces, youthful healthy bodies. He saw them in church when he felt like going and then he'd heard they were planning a New Year's get-together at the tavern.

It had seemed like a golden opportunity to stop dreaming and start enjoying his fantasies in real life. He was good at planning, too. He'd even managed to slip them just enough of the drug that they'd been able to get out to their car and start driving home.

It would have been hopeless if they'd passed out in the bar. Instead they had grown cautious because they weren't feeling well and finally had drifted off the road as easily as they fell asleep.

A great plan, one leaving no tracks that would lead to him. But the first one had proved to be a mistake, and now the other two had been in that basement for so long that the smell was sour when he opened the storm doors.

He wasn't sure he even wanted them anymore.

Yeah, they could shower, but that wasn't going to put meat back on them. At his last check a few days ago, they'd looked almost like skeletons.

He didn't find them attractive anymore. What was he going to do? Drag their submissive, weakened butts out of the hole and fatten them up again? Hoping they'd be grateful to him? That they wouldn't act like the first one once they got a little energy back?

Much as he hated to admit it, despite everything he'd done right, he'd messed up. He should never have taken all three at once. He shouldn't have done it so close to home, not when a so-called friend like Spence was going to shoot off his mouth.

He tried to tell himself that Spence had merely diverted attention with his behavior. After all, no cop would expect the kidnapper to draw attention to himself.

But maybe that wasn't true. Maybe the guilty often liked to needle the cops. Hell, he'd read about how many guys had been caught simply because they couldn't avoid going back to the scene of the crime to watch. To enjoy their own handiwork.

He for sure wasn't that dumb. Hence finding a place far enough away, long enough abandoned, that it didn't look as if anything could possibly live in there except some rats and ground squirrels. It wasn't even on his property. No one could conceivably know that he'd shored up the root cellar to make a small prison.

He hadn't even had to buy any materials for the job. His long-gone family had left enough crap in his barn that he could probably build an ark for Noah. The thought amused him while the TV, with a snowy picture as usual, blathered on about how bad the storm was going to be.

At least he didn't have to go to work at the garage. His boss, Keeb Dustin, had told him to stay home. After the storm they'd probably work around the clock trying to jump-start dead batteries and repair bent fenders and snapped belts. The cold, this kind of cold, was cruel to cars.

And then there'd be the tows. A lot of people might well get stuck trying to get out of their own driveways, especially outside town. Or stuck in ditches because it was a strange fact that every single year people needed to learn to drive on snow all over again, and this would be the first snow this year.

So yeah, he'd be plenty busy for a few days after the storm. He might even pick up a few hours driving a plow if they got really buried.

Which left the girls. And leaving them was just about what he'd convinced himself to do. Too much trouble. Try another time. Learn from this and move on.

Hell, the cold from this storm would probably kill them in a few hours, and damned if he was going to drag them out of their hiding places and bring them here. Just his luck some cop, like that Kelly Noveno, would stop by to check on him and one of those damn teens would start screaming her fool head off.

Leave them, he thought. Let nature take care of them.

There were plenty more where they came from.

AL TURNED IN the scrap of cloth he'd found while rescuing Ruffles and Gage slipped it into an evidence bag with tweezers before looking it over. "Did you record where you found this?"

Al pulled out his cell phone and showed him the information. "I got it all, including the GPS, but I don't know what good it does us."

"Maybe nothing yet. Maybe nothing ever. But one of those girls was wearing a pink parka when she disappeared and this appears to be the right kind of nylon fabric. Then look, did you see the teeth marks?"

Astonished, Al leaned forward for a closer look. "It was chewed," he said.

"Yeah, it was. Which is an odd thing to do with one's parka, I have to say. Looks like it was deliberately ripped off."

Al's heart stuttered to full speed. "Maybe I should look around some more near Mrs. Jackson's. I didn't see any buildings anywhere near but…"

Gage nodded. "Wind," he said. "It's light-weight." Then he motioned Al over to a wall map of the county, one that was decorated with pushpins. "Here's Mrs. Jackson's place. Nearest structure is probably…five miles? There might be some old line shacks out there, but nothing that's occupied. Wouldn't hurt to look around some, if you feel like it."

Then Al's radio clamored for his attention. A family of felines had been dumped by the state highway, spotted by a trucker who couldn't stop for them. "I've gotta go," he told Gage.

"Yeah. I'll think about this," he said, indicating the swatch of fabric. "Maybe something will come to me."

"It better come soon. That storm is supposed to hit tomorrow night or the next morning."

Gage merely nodded. Because, of course, he already knew.

KELLY WATCHED THE sky thicken with threat and was glad she was out doing the rest of the welfare checks. The predictions for the storm had grown so much worse that sometimes entire families were telling her they were moving into town to stay with relatives and friends, or at one of the church shelters.

Few wanted to be caught out here if something went wrong. One grizzled rancher wanted a few minutes of conversation and she was happy to provide it.

"Can't go into town," he said. "I got me some forty cows in the barn I gotta look after. Thank the good Lord I could get them all in."

"Can someone stay with you?"

He laughed. "I'm moving in with the cows. They'll keep me warm as toast and I'll have ice cream fresh from the tap."

She joined his laughter. "It *is* going to be bad."

"I reckon." He looked up at the sky. "You can laugh if you want, Deputy Kelly, but I'll tell you anyway. Spent my whole life out here. This ain't normal weather we been having, not for a few years now. And this storm? Nothing like it ever before. Them folks can laugh at climate change all they want, but I'm living close to it and I see it. It's not the same, not the way it was. So let 'em tell me it's just one storm and doesn't mean a hill of beans."

They probably would say exactly that, she thought as she drove away with a wave. Not everyone, but some. She'd been listening to the arguments for a long time now. She did, however, listen to her dad.

"Streets are flooding all the time down here, Kelly. Never used to see that. Houses that were safe except in the worst hurricanes are getting flooded at high tide, especially if we've had some rain. Streets undrivable. Things are changing. I'm glad you're up there."

Things are changing. Maybe that was the only thing people would agree on. But behind her Bugle let out a low moan, reminding her she hadn't given him a chance to take care of his business for a while now.

"Bad, bad Kelly," she said aloud. In the rearview, she could see Bugle cock his head inquisitively. "Next turnout," she promised him. It'd give her a chance to give the binoculars on the seat beside her a good workout. At every opportunity she'd scanned the surrounding country because she couldn't stop hoping she'd find some sign of the missing teens.

The rabbit in her house seemed like a minor thing compared with that. So somebody wanted to make her uneasy. Big deal. They probably also didn't want to mess with Bugle. She didn't need the Glock on her hip to feel safe.

But unless those girls were being held somewhere right around here, hope was nearly pointless. They were gone, one way or another, maybe not even in this county anymore. And if someone was holding them prisoner somewhere around here…well, something should give him away soon. A trip to a store, a pharmacy, extra food… if he had to care for three teens, he was going to need supplies. Supplies that wouldn't be on his usual shopping list.

Maybe.

But so far nobody had come to the sheriff remarking that they'd noticed something unusual. The most unusual thing had been that dolt Spence poking at her, and that hadn't been the first time she'd run into a jerk who liked to give a cop a hard time.

In fact, given the kidnapping, she was surprised that she and other cops hadn't suffered a whole lot more from impatient, angry people. They must seem like total failures.

And from Kelly's perspective, she felt like one. It seemed next to impossible that someone could have taken those girls and left no evidence behind. That was one of the almost unbreakable rules of crime scene investigation: take something, leave something behind.

But if he'd left anything behind, they didn't know what it was. They might stare straight at it and not know it. That glove was all they had. It linked to one of the girls, but not to the perp. No help until they had someone to charge.

Sometimes she found that the most frustrating part of police work, to be able to develop a mountain of evidence that you couldn't link to anyone specific until you put hands on the guy.

How many men in this county—assuming it was a man—might be enough of a pervert to take those girls? Did any of them have families they were hiding this from? Or did they all live alone? How many of *them* were there, solitary men?

Plenty, unfortunately. Women seemed more eager to leave this town and county than men by far. They wanted something more than the smell of cow poop and skunk in the morning.

She found a turnout and let Bugle out without a leash. He needed to run off some energy. Then she pulled out the binoculars and began to scan the countryside from east to west toward the mountains. A tumbledown line shack that looked like it should have collapsed long ago. No houses immediately in sight, but yeah, she thought she could see one farther out. A couple of miles? Possibly next on her checklist.

The mountains, for all they had prepared for winter, still looked dark and forbidding, probably because the sky was trying to work itself into an early version of night with lowering clouds.

The air felt oddly warm, though. Strange, but maybe it was an effect of the approaching cold, sucking heat toward it from somewhere else. Her weather knowledge was miserable, but as she stood there studying the barren countryside and a few cattle that really needed to be on their way into a barn, she wondered if she should have majored in meteorology.

Following in her father's footsteps had seemed like the thing to do for so many years, but how often had Hector tried to talk her out of it?

"You don't know, *muchacha*," he'd say to her. "The things we have to see. I'm not talking about risks. Sure there are risks but it's more dangerous to cut down trees or catch crabs. No, I'm talking about what we *see*. Things that get stamped in the brain and never go away. Why would you want to do that?"

Because that's what he had done and she admired the heck out of him. He'd been right about the things stamped in her brain, however. Absolutely right. At least she saw a lot fewer of them here in Wyoming than she had during her brief stint in Fort Lauderdale.

When Bugle apparently felt he'd run off enough energy, he came back to her with his tail wagging, ready to go on patrol again. It seemed he hadn't noticed anything untoward, and only then did she realize how much she'd been hoping that he'd find another piece of evidence, like that glove.

No such luck. She put him back in his cage in the backseat and wondered absently how soon it would get so cold that she'd need to put his quilted vest and booties on him. Not yet, anyway.

By comparison with the last few days, the air felt almost balmy.

Before she pulled back out onto the road, her cell phone tweeted at her. She almost laughed. She thought she'd been out of range for a while.

"Hey," said the now-familiar voice of Al Carstairs, "how are your rounds going?"

"Nearly done, for today at any rate. You?"

"Couple more houses. I'll be out on 581 for the next half hour or so. Listen, when you want lunch, look me up. I've got a story about a Maine coon for you, and I found a scrap of pink cloth that even Gage isn't sure means anything."

"Pretend you just heard me sigh. Okay, I'll see you on 581. Maybe an hour?"

"I'll be there. I'm running back to my cabin first, though. Some people call me on the land-line and talk to my answering machine. Can you believe it? An answering machine in this day and age."

She laughed. "Hey, you heard of voice mail?"

"County won't pay for the additional service. Nope, I'm a tape man. Play and erase. See you shortly."

A Maine coon and a good story. Sounded like it might be a nice lunch break. Plus a piece of fabric. Her heart did one of those nervous little skips it had been doing ever since this case exploded.

She closed her eyes a few moments, sending a prayer for those girls winging heavenward, then pulled back onto the road.

She believed in a benevolent God. Absolutely. But she also figured the human race had him or her so overworked that single prayers might get lost in the tsunami.

"We make most of our own problems," her father had told her once. She wasn't sure if he was speaking as a cop or a dad, nor did it really matter. They'd just come out of Mass, and she'd donated her babysitting money to the poor.

"What do you mean?" she'd asked him.

"People don't starve because God wants it. They starve because other people are hard-hearted."

That philosophy had stuck. So maybe her prayer was useless. A bad guy was involved in all this. He had made this problem. Unfortunately, entirely too many people were in the perp's class, harming others for their own satisfaction.

But that didn't keep her from saying yet another prayer as she drove.

Back at his cabin, Al got word of two missing cats, and he still had the ones dropped by the roadside to worry about. Kittens. If he hurried up, he could grab them and get to 581 with the missing cats who'd been out since last night.

Cats were a piece of work, he sometimes thought. He loved them as much as any animals, but cats could be especially difficult. Somehow, they'd managed to keep their own minds and wills intact. They could be cuddly companions one minute and troublesome isolationists the next.

As he jumped back into his truck, ready to rescue the local feline population, he felt a light weight land on his shoulder.

"Regis," he said, twisting his head to look at the gray squirrel. "You really don't want to come along to look for cats."

But Regis, like the cats, had his own mind. He chittered, then settled into the space between Al's collar and shoulder.

And that, thought Al, was what he got for rescuing an infant squirrel last spring and nursing him to health before releasing him. Regis still had a bit of human in him.

FIFTEEN MINUTES LATER he'd rescued the family of cats, the kittens no more than a week old, and placed them on a towel together in a cage in the back of his truck. Mama immediately wrapped herself around them, protecting them. The two other missing cats showed up on their home porches, so he erased them from his mental list.

Once he approached 581 he saw Salty, a schnauzer from an outlying ranch that shouldn't be anywhere around here. So Salty was placed in a cage a distance from the cats and began to whine. Of course. He'd probably been having a great time chasing a ground squirrel, had indeed chased it so far he was too far from home.

At last he turned onto 581, looking forward to seeing Kelly. She was occupying a whole lot more time in his thoughts than was probably good for him, but he was past caring. There were enough bad things to think about.

Kelly was like a bright shining oasis in a world full of ugliness.

Then he spied Misty. A beautiful golden retriever with a distinctive prance to her step, she seemed to be running in circles about a hundred yards inside the fence line of the Harris family ranch. He was surprised to see her so far out here. The Avilas had always been careful owners who tried not to let Misty slip her leash, but she was an accomplished escape artist. With the weather turning so bitter, perhaps one of the kids had let her out in the backyard without watching and she'd burrowed under the fence. Regardless, at the times she proved to be Houdini's reincarnation, Al usually picked her up within or near the city limits.

Al pulled his van onto the shoulder, grabbed a slipknot leash and climbed out. Misty had never been a problem to round up, so he expected her to come immediately when he called. Just after he slid off the seat and his feet hit the ground, he felt Regis dig in his claws. He had to smile.

He closed the vehicle door so the animals would stay warm and gave thanks that the wind hadn't really started yet. Just the faintest of breezes had begun to chill the air, starting to vanquish the unusual warmth of the last few hours, and now held a tang that hinted at coming snow.

For the first time ever, Misty wasn't in a co-operative mood. As she raced around, she tossed some kind of toy in the air, and although she occasionally glanced at him when he called her, she kept right on playing, pausing only to paw at the ground before returning to her private game of catch.

"Hey, Misty," Al called. "Come on. Don't be a pain. Seriously."

Just then a sheriff's SUV pulled onto the opposite shoulder of the road. It bore a rack of lights, and Conard County Sheriff painted in green on the tan background. K-9, Keep Your Distance was also labeled on the side. By that, before she even climbed out, Al knew it was Kelly.

She had apparently taken in the situation before she pulled over to approach him, and grinned as she climbed out. "Having a problem, Al?"

He had to grin back. Kelly was a wildly attractive woman to his way of thinking, but what he most liked about her was her sunny nature and readiness to tease. He also liked her dog, but Kelly left Bugle in her vehicle and sauntered toward Al, her khaki uniform and jacket looking scarcely heavy enough to withstand the chilling air. "Misty giving you trouble?"

"She's in a mood, all right," Al agreed. Apparently, Kelly had had her own run-ins with the dog.

Kelly whistled, but Misty barely spared her a glance as she tossed her toy in the air and caught it.

"What in the world is she playing with?" Kelly asked.

"I've been wondering. Rawhide bone? Heck, she knows I wouldn't take that away from her."

Kelly chuckled. "She's teasing you." Then she turned to look at Al. "What in the dickens is that on your shoulder?"

Al didn't even have to glance. "That's Regis."

"That's a *squirrel*! You can't keep them for pets."

"I don't. Regis decides for himself. Sometimes he likes to ride shotgun. What can I tell you, Kelly? The squirrel has a mind of his own."

Al felt her staring but heck, what could he do about it? He'd rescued Regis as an abandoned baby, fed the animal until it was strong enough to take off into the woods and live the squirrel life. Except Regis kept coming back to visit.

"Now I've seen everything," Kelly muttered. "Someday I want to hear this story."

While Al wouldn't have minded spending the next day or two chatting with Kelly, there was still business to attend to. "Misty, get your butt over here now." This time there was an edge of impatience to his voice and Misty didn't miss it. She froze, looked at him, then came trotting over with her toy.

Al squatted down, ready to reward the dog with a good scratch and rub, but as Misty drew closer something inside him began to feel chillier than the day.

"Kelly?"

"That's not rawhide," she said too quietly.

Al didn't answer. He waited until Misty snaked through the fence and came to a halt before him, dropping her toy and looking at him with a proud grin.

Al reached out, scratching her neck automatically as he looked down at the "present" she'd placed before him.

"Tell me that's not human," he said.

"I can't," Kelly answered, her voice unusually taut.

Their eyes met and Al knew they were both thinking of the same thing: the three high school girls who'd gone missing weeks ago.

"I'll get an evidence bag while you put the dog in your van," Kelly said. But he noted she walked to her SUV with a leaden step. All her natural vivacity had seeped away. She'd be calling for help, he thought, to try to learn where the dog found the bone. Before they were even certain.

"Yeah," Al said, speaking to the icy air. "Yeah."

Then he stood, slipping the loose leash around Misty and leading her to the back of his truck.

"God," he told the dog, "I hope it's from a deer."

But he was very afraid it was not.

Chapter Eleven

Days 20–21

An hour later, Cadel Marcus showed up with four of the K-9s he was training, and Jake wasn't far behind with his dog. Soon deputies began to congregate, filling the shoulders of the road, cutting it off to traffic.

The only thing they knew for sure was that a doctor at the hospital had said it was definitely a human thighbone, the growth plates hadn't fully hardened and he wouldn't be surprised if it belonged to one of the missing girls. The bone was now on its way to a forensics lab, but there was no time to waste.

Gage was blunt about it. "Figure we've got twenty-four hours max," he told everyone. "We've got to find the scene, find the body, find the evidence before this storm makes working impossible, or buries the remains again."

And none of that meant they'd find the perp.

Al had used the time to take the animals in

his truck home or leave them in his kennels, and now he was ready to take one of Cadel's dogs to aid in the search.

"Same commands you've heard Kelly use with Bugle," Cadel told him. "Except these dogs are trained to hunt for cadaverine."

Cadaverine. The odor of death, something dogs could sniff even if it was way more than six feet underground. "Bugle doesn't do that?"

"Around here, not much call. Three of these dogs are in training for other police departments. One body hunter is probably all we'd ordinarily need in this county. Today is different."

Different in so many ways, with a severe storm moving in that could hide evidence until much later in the spring. That would give scavengers more time to devour it and disperse it. Important traces, like cloth and hair, could vanish in a strong wind. Even teeth…

Al drew himself up short. He'd seen it in Afghanistan. He didn't need to think about all the stages of decay.

Kelly approached him, her face drawn. "I'd like to miss this day entirely."

"I think we all would," he agreed. "I'm sorry. I had funny stories to tell you."

"Where's that damn squirrel of yours?"

"Being smart. When I got back to my place, he headed for his drey. I don't know if he made himself a family yet, but I'm sure he's got other squirrels to hunker down with."

"I definitely want to hear that story."

"You will."

As if they were hunting for someone buried in a landslide or avalanche, they all carried long, thin metal poles to stick into the hardened ground. It wasn't easy, but they were thin enough to penetrate with reasonable effort. Even so, Al felt it all the way through his injured back.

But what they all really wanted was for the dogs to alert. To give them a narrower area to search.

They set out almost shoulder to shoulder, heading toward the area where Misty had been playing with the bone. Unfortunately, Misty had probably found it somewhere else and had carried it with her while she played.

Cadel had spread his dogs out with other deputies so they covered a much wider area. They offered more hope than rods and eyes right now. At least they still had visibility, but it seemed like the winter night was moving in even faster than usual. Al wished he had some night vision goggles. Detail was beginning to vanish as the light grew flatter by the minute.

Even if they found remains, all they could do was cover them until morning and hope it didn't grow too cold for the crime scene folks to gather everything in the morning light.

But mostly Al thought about the girl that bone had belonged to, about all three of the missing girls. How awful all the way around, from their disappearance to their parents' hoping and praying they'd be found alive to this.

He doubted anyone wanted to tell the parents about the bone. It might not belong to one of the girls. It could have come from somewhere else. Why terrify them any more than they were already terrified. Why steal the hope they had been depending on for weeks now.

Not without damn good reason.

But for him, as for many of the searchers, he suspected, hope was clinging by one last, thin thread after the bone. No reason to think only one of the girls had been killed. That would make no sense at all.

Not that any of this made any sense.

The wind was picking up as the last light faded from the day. They were done until first light in the morning. The dogs hadn't even signaled, and Al was quite sure they'd long since passed the spot where Misty had been playing. The question now was where she had found it.

They marked the place where they stopped looking with pin flags, then tramped dispiritedly back to the cars. For some reason, a hope of another kind had been born in the searchers: hope of closure. Even that was denied to them tonight.

Back at his car he saw Kelly loading up Bugle. He turned his charge back over to Cadel and headed her way.

"Say, Deputy," he said. The wind tried to snatch his words.

She looked at him, her expression sober, her hand on the driver's door latch.

"Come to my place tonight," he said. "It's a good night for not being alone."

To his amazement, she nodded. "I'd like that. Bugle, too?"

"I can't imagine you without that dog. Of course he comes."

She smiled lopsidedly. "Do you need me to bring anything?"

"Yourself and your dog. The pizza place is on the way if that agrees with you."

"I love pizza. Any kind, except anchovies. They're too salty for me."

"Done. See you there shortly. And oh, by the way? I have food for Bugle, too, so just bring something warm to hang out in. I have a feeling the temperatures tonight will make the North Pole seem balmy."

In fact they were already headed that way, he thought as he climbed into his truck. He really needed to check the weather so they'd know what they were facing tomorrow.

Of course, the weather was going to be only a small part of it.

KELLY PACKED HER usual flannel pajamas, slippers and robe, as well as a fresh set of silky thermal underwear for the morning, a clean uniform and Bugle's tug rope. From the way the air was feeling outside, she wasn't sure this storm was going to wait until the day after tomorrow.

So when they started in at dawn, they were going to have to give the search a massive effort. If only Misty could show them where she'd found the bone. Of course, any carrion eater could have dragged it away from the rest of the body. Whoever the poor victim was, he or she could be scattered over acres by now.

The pressure of time rode her like a goad. The coming storm could hamper them so much, could blow away evidence, could even bury things and freeze them so hard that the best dog might have trouble picking out a scent.

Maybe that had been part of their problem this afternoon. The body had been frozen, had lost a great many of its scents, those scents had been overlaid by whatever animals had torn at the flesh…

Cold as it was, a corpse should have been preserved, but not in the open where coyotes, bears, mountain lions and even wolves could get to it. Food was in short supply and high demand in the cold of winter. And bears, while they hibernated, often emerged from their dens in the course of the winter to hunt for food, as well. If there were easy pickings…

She didn't want to think about it. They couldn't do much until morning. At this point an air sweep probably wouldn't find a thing. Why should it? It hadn't directly after the girls had gone missing. No brightly colored clothing had given them away then, so why expect it now when the elements and the animals had had their way?

With her carryall packed, she hesitated, looking around her little house for anything she might have forgotten. The heat was on, the water was dripping so pipes wouldn't freeze, and she could think of nothing else she needed.

She and Bugle climbed into her official vehicle, which she'd left running, and a blast of warm air from the heater thawed her cheeks, which had started to freeze on the way out the door. Colder and colder.

Cold weather was nothing new here, but this was going to be a killer cold if the forecast was correct, maybe hitting thirty or forty below. That wasn't a regular event. Sure it happened sometimes in the winter, but compared with places farther north, this part of Wyoming was usually much gentler.

Regardless of what was *usual*, the approaching storm was going to be a winter beast and would curtail them in their search for a body and evidence. Every minute tomorrow was going to count.

Al's cabin and kennels took up a couple of acres about five miles away from town along a paved county road. A big wooden sign, deeply carved and recently painted, announced that this was Conard County Animal Control, Chief Allan Carstairs. Two phone numbers, in smaller lettering, filled the bottom.

His driveway was in fairly good shape, given the time of year and that it was gravel, and soon she was pulling up to his front door and parking beside his van and his truck with the high cab on the bed to make room for cages.

Sitting out front was a cute wood cutout of a dog and a cat looking welcoming. She wondered if Al had created them.

The cabin itself, while looking like a leftover from the frontier days, was in great shape and the light pouring from windows was inviting. Smoke, caught in the gleam of her headlights, rose from a chimney. He must have built a fire.

It was almost as if all the bad things that had been riding her shoulders lifted and drifted away. There was nothing to be done tonight except enjoy time with a man she had come to like a whole lot more than she probably should.

Plus, tonight she wouldn't have to sit in her own house counting on Bugle's protection. Because whether she wanted to admit it or not, the stuffed rabbit had unnerved her. Someone had entered her house for no discernible reason and left behind a toy that might have been wearing a bow but might also have been wearing a noose.

She'd have to be made of steel not to be uneasy about that. Nor could she imagine any possible reason for it. Who the hell did *she* threaten?

Well, she had a night off from that, too. Maybe when the whole case got sorted out, she'd find out what that rabbit meant along with all the rest of it.

Then Al opened the front door, a powerful silhouette against the light behind, and waved her to come in.

For the first time in hours, she genuinely smiled. Sight for sore eyes, she thought. Bugle even gave a woof of approval.

Yeah, they'd made the right decision to accept his invitation.

REVE CAME BACK from checking on the girls. It would be his last check. He figured the coming cold would kill them, but since he wasn't entirely heartless, he'd left them some more water and food bars. Lucky the cold had put them to sleep or he wouldn't have left them anything.

Then he headed back to his place, headlights out as always, beneath a sky that had been blotted by clouds until he was practically driving into a black hole. Only once he was on the county road again did he turn his lights back on.

Nobody flying tonight. Nobody searching tonight. He felt free as a bird.

Until he got home and his landline rang. It was Spence.

"What do you want?" he asked irritably. Spence was an okay friend to have at the tavern, but Reve didn't much care for socializing in general. He'd go to church once in a while, smile at a few old ladies and grab some baked goods. The baked goods were free and were always delicious, and the old biddies pressed him to take loads because he was so thin.

Lean and mean more like, he always told himself. But he wouldn't turn down a whole pie, or an entire plate of brownies.

But friends? They had to be kept in their proper places, and Spence's proper place was at the tavern, at the pool table. Besides, he was mad at Spence for giving that deputy a hard time.

Cripes, a man on probation ought to know better.

"Hey," said Spence, "you see all the excitement of them looking for those gals this afternoon? Did you hear about the bone?"

Now Reve no longer felt like hanging up. Spence had piqued his attention. "What bone?"

"Story is some dog found it and was playing with it. Deputy Dawg took it to the hospital and they identified it as a human thighbone. You should have seen the show. They were out there for hours this afternoon with searchers and dogs. Didn't find anything."

Reve tried to decide if that was good or bad. "Sounds bad," he said finally, though he didn't mean it.

"Well, I had my fun."

"What fun?"

"You know the cars them gals was drivin'? Before Deputy Dawg came along I found it. Nothing inside. I was hoping for a wallet. Instead I found a damned stuffed rabbit. I brought it home to give to my dog for a toy, then decided to have some fun."

Reve's stomach had begun to knot. "What kind of fun?"

"I left it at the deputy's house. Only seemed right. They can't find them missing gals, and after the look she gave me at the tavern when I said something about it, I thought I'd give her a little fright."

"You said you'd left part of an animal skin!"

"Fooled ya," Spence laughed.

Reve swore. "Let me guess. You left your fingerprints all over the toy and her house!"

"Man, I ain't no fool. Had too many brushes with the law. Nah, I wore gloves. Jeez, it's cold out there. Everybody's wearing gloves. Like I'd grab something like that with my bare hands, or use them to leave it at Noveno's house. Give me some credit, Reve."

Oh, Reve gave him credit, all right. Credit for being the biggest fool to ever walk on two legs. Taunting the deputy hadn't been enough. No, he had to go drop a big fat threat at her doorstep. "If you get picked up again, blame yourself."

Spence snorted. "No way on earth they can find out it was me. Wish I'd got to the car earlier, though. I wish I'd seen what happened to those girls."

You're lucky you didn't, Reve thought as he hung up his phone. Although at this point he was wondering if Spence wasn't a liability he needed to get rid of, the sooner the better.

But how?

He sat at his table, oil and whetting stone in front of him as he followed his monthly ritual of sharpening the kitchen knives. The process soothed him, and he enjoyed seeing how the blades had worn away with time, becoming narrower but no less sharp. When he finished each one, he would wipe the oil from it and test his arm to make sure it was sharp enough to cut the hair from him, like a razor. Better than a razor.

For now, he forgot about the girls. They were rapidly passing into the rearview mirror of his life, little to interest him, soon to be gone. Their bones might be found in a century or two.

But the other one, the one he had taken out to

the gully and covered with tumbleweed. A bone. So the animals had done their work, but that meant that the cops had renewed their search.

And Spence had just put his ham-fisted "joke" in the middle of it all. Damn, if those cops started taking a close look at that rabbit, they might find something from one of the girls on it. A hair. Whatever. And Spence in his absolute idiocy had thought it would be funny to try to scare the deputy with it, sure in his folly that no link would ever be made to anything.

The regular grating sound of the metal on the whetting stone created a comforting rhythm, but Reve wasn't comforted at all. Damn Spence, he might have created a serious problem for him. No, there was nothing that should link Reve to the girls, but the rabbit… How had he overlooked the rabbit when he pulled everything out of the car? What if it had *Reve's* hair on it? Just because he'd been wearing a watch cap didn't mean strands of his hair weren't elsewhere, ready to fall off him like mini grenades.

Crap, that thought really disturbed him. There he'd been trying to be so careful and only *now* did it occur to him that there might have been a stray hair or two on his jacket or jeans?

Not that it mattered unless they caught him. He'd never been arrested, nobody had his DNA that he knew of…

He twisted on the chair, putting the knife

down, and reached into the fridge for another longneck. He was worrying too much. The girls would be gone, nobody would find them for a hundred years. Think how much harder he'd have made it on himself if he'd tried to bring them here and make them behave. Nah, that first girl had taught him a lesson. He just hadn't taken it far enough.

Next time, he'd know better how to accomplish this. And he'd start with one girl at a time.

AL'S LIVING ROOM was hardly any bigger than her own, and it, too, had a kitchen in one corner, except he didn't have a bar as a divider.

A fire burned warmly on a fieldstone hearth, adding cheery light and warmth. As he took her bag and leaned it nearby against a log wall, she turned slowly to look. Yes, it was a log cabin, but the whole feel of it, dark wood and all, made it seem so cozy, much more so than her house, which she had already thought was cozy.

Then she spied a small white Christmas tree in the corner near the front door and wide window. She couldn't help smiling.

"I know," he said, as if reading her mind. "It's still there. But some nights I just like to light it up and watch it change colors. It's fiber optic with one of those color wheels."

"Red and green?"

"Nah. More pastel. If you like, I'll show you later. But while the pizza is still warm…"

He'd gotten a pie with everything except anchovies. Maybe he'd made the store put extra veggies and pepperoni on it, because she couldn't remember seeing one loaded with so many green peppers, onions and mushrooms.

Two plates sat beside the box, and he served her a piece, inviting her to sit on his sofa. He actually had a sofa. But before he served himself, he opened a kitchen cupboard and pulled out a rawhide bone for Bugle. He looked at Kelly. "Is it okay for me to give this to him?"

She appreciated his understanding of the bond between her and Bugle that had to be protected, but it didn't need to be protected every single second.

Bugle knew exactly what Al was holding, and sat at attention, his mouth framing his version of an eager smile.

"Bugle, okay." At once the dog trotted over to Al and quickly accepted the gift. Al grinned.

The dog decided this place was okay and the offering pleased him. Soon he was sprawled on a colorful area rug, gnawing intently and happily.

Al joined her on the sofa with his plate. "TV might be hard to come by. They never ran the cable all the way out here, but I have a dish. I use it mostly for internet, but I can get a few stations if you're in the mood. Otherwise I have a collection of movies that ought to embarrass me."

"Why?"

"Because every time I think about how much I've spent on DVDs, I think how much healthier my bank account could look."

She laughed, then took a bite of her pie. "This is great. What magic wand did you use?"

"A credit card that was willing to pay for extra toppings. I mean, I like the sauce and cheese well enough, but it's the toppings I'm really after."

"One piece will be an entire meal!"

He winked. "For you, maybe." Plate in hand, he rose from the couch and walked over to his little Christmas tree. It wasn't very large, just over three feet, but when he flipped a switch it became a gorgeous panoply of slowly changing lights. To her delight, she thought the nearly pastel colors were prettier than the usual Christmas colors.

"There," he said, returning to her side. "A little ambience. We could sure use some. Today was tough."

In so many ways. The bone, a virtual guarantee that at least one of the girls was dead. As for the other two...

Kelly sighed and closed her eyes. A moment later she started as she felt a weight on her thigh. Opening her eyes, she saw Al's hand.

"Don't stop eating. I shouldn't have mentioned

it. Even on the battlefield we took breaks when we could. Otherwise you go nuts or become useless."

He probably had a point, she thought. It was hard to shed the feeling of wasted time, of guilt, but there was nothing they could do out there tonight. It was dangerously cold. How many people did they want to put in the hospital from frostbite or hypothermia when they didn't even have a definite place to look?

If only they could ask Misty where she'd found that bone, but the dog wasn't likely to learn to talk. Then she had a thought and sat bolt upright.

"What?" Al asked immediately.

"Misty," she said. "What if we took her back out there? She might want to find another bone to play with. If they were close enough, she might be able to guide us to others."

He nodded slowly, evidently thinking about it. "It might work. She was sure having fun with it, and a dog would remember where there were others."

"I never had a dog lose a rawhide bone. Hide it maybe, lose it never."

"I think we should try it. I'll give the Avilas a call in the morning and ask to borrow Misty. Better clear it with the sheriff, too, I guess."

Her appetite was coming back and just before she took a bite of pizza, she said, "I think

Gage would try anything that had even a remote chance of helping."

"I'd walk barefoot on desert sand right now. I think he's probably feeling about the same."

"I know I am."

She managed to finish the slice, but her mind was wandering down the rabbit hole again. What if she'd found the car a little earlier? What if she'd looked a little closer for some evidence? Why hadn't she been more suspicious?

That was really killing her, that she'd treated a car in the ditch as a matter of no importance once she found that no one was in it and hurt. While that might have been true most of the time, it sure as hell hadn't been that night.

God!

But even so, she wasn't sure what she might have done differently. She'd been beating her head on that wall since the instant she learned that three young women had been in that car and that all of them were missing.

What *could* she have done differently? She didn't even know who was involved. She'd called the phone number on the registration and left a message when there was no answer. It wasn't as if she could have even done a thing to raise the alarm earlier.

Fingers snapped in front of her. Startled, she drew back a little and looked at Al. "What?"

"Come out of that hole you're digging. It's

not going to help anything at all, Kelly. Beating yourself up is no help either. I should know."

She shook her head a little, but he wouldn't let her look away. He placed his finger beneath her chin and turned her head toward him. His gray eyes had grown distant and dark, like windows on hell.

"I was on a mission. Afghanistan. We were supposed to be training a local unit in mountain patrols. Unfortunately, we trusted the wrong people. I lost two men. Two. Our supposed allies turned on us, right when we were vulnerable because we were supposed to be working together. You wanna know how many weeks I spent beating myself up over that?"

She drew a long breath, unable to look away now. He was sharing something deeply personal and painful, and deserved her full attention. Her heart felt as if it were squeezing in her chest. So much anguish, so carefully controlled.

"There should have been a clue, I thought. I should have seen some sign that they were plotting, that they weren't trustworthy, that they meant us harm. How in the hell could I have eaten with them, joked with them, traipsed shoulder to shoulder with them on that patrol and never, *never* picked up on any warning sign?"

"Al…" she breathed.

"Yeah," he said after a few beats. "I know that hole you're digging. I've plumbed it all the way to the bottom. Thing is, I never got an answer. I just kept hating myself until another officer who'd gone through the same thing finally asked me, 'Are you supposed to be psychic? Prescient? None of us is that. None.' I got his point. It was a while before I could let go, and I still get angry, but I've had to accept I didn't do anything *wrong*." His gaze lost a bit of its edge. "You didn't do anything wrong either. Get used to it. It'll never feel good, but the guilt is wasted. You did everything right."

She had a feeling it might be a while before she'd be able to believe that, but she could accept what he was saying about not digging herself into a deep hole. Beating herself up hadn't done a bit of good so far. Not one little bit.

He stirred, setting his plate aside on an end table, then scooted over until he could wrap his arm around her shoulders and draw her into a loose but comforting embrace. "I can't dictate the best way for you to handle this," he said quietly. "We're all different and I'm no shrink. But I honestly feel that you didn't do anything wrong. Not easy to live with, but not everything is easy. Especially stuff like this."

She placed her plate on the arm of the sofa and turned into him, enjoying the warmth and strength of his embrace, only in those moments realizing how *lonely* she'd been feeling in the past few weeks. His scents, of the outdoors, of man, filled her, touching her deeply in ways she hadn't felt in a long time.

Yeah, she was surrounded by comrades who'd joined the search, but she still felt alone, probably because she'd been the one to find the car. No one else had to deal with that.

But Al understood, and he was offering comfort. And while she tried to remain strong at all times, she could remember tears in her own father's eyes from time to time, and it didn't seem like weakness to accept the comfort Al was offering.

He tightened his arm around her shoulders just a bit, making her feel more secure, letting her know that she was welcome. Resting her head on his chest, she listened to his strong, steady heartbeat and watched the play of firelight and his silly little fiber-optic tree. It felt almost as if she'd stepped into some kind of dream.

Another world, one far away from her worries of the past few weeks. Could it be so bad to take a break for just one evening, especially when the temperature was dropping dramatically outside and no one could possibly continue the search?

The sight of Bugle happily gnawing on his rawhide added to the feeling of contentment that was trying to rise in her, offering her that break she probably needed. No reason to feel guilty. No reason to beat her head on the problem until morning. She said another prayer for the girls out there and hoped that they'd finally get a break in the morning. But until then…

Al murmured her name.

At once she lifted her head and looked at him.

"I'm no good at this," he said, brushing a strand of hair back from her face.

"At what?"

"I told you. Relationships. But…" Almost as if an invisible force tugged them together, their faces came close and their mouths met. At first it was a tentative kiss, a feeling-out, but not for long. Kelly reached up a hand to cradle the back of his head and draw him closer, to deepen the kiss that soon grew hard and demanding.

Oh, man, it had been too long, she thought. Entirely too long because of all her scruples about her job but all those scruples seemed to be vanishing before the force of her need for this man.

This one man, not just any man, she realized hazily as her body began to awaken to desire long suppressed. Man, she should have jumped his bones ages ago. The idea nearly drew a giggle from her.

Apparently he felt it because he pulled back a little, letting her catch her breath. "What's funny?"

She could feel her cheeks heat. She hoped he thought it was the heat from the fireplace, although it wasn't *that* warm. "It's silly," she said, sounding as if she had to force the words out.

"Oh. That's okay. I always thought you were the most wildly beautiful woman I'd ever seen."

Wildly beautiful? Her heart slammed and began a rapid tap dance of delight. "I was just thinking…" She drew a breath and blurted it. Truth for truth. "I was just thinking I should have jumped your bones a long time ago."

The smile that spread over his face would have lit the arctic night brighter than the aurora. "Oh, I do like the sound of that."

With a gentle hand, he cupped her cheek and drew her in for another kiss. "Jump away," he murmured against her lips. "Anytime."

She was falling into him, all wariness and reluctance fading away, her world becoming Al Carstairs. Everything else vanished as her body felt a new tide rising, a tide of need and longing, a tsunami of desire long denied. It was washing through her and over her and driving out everything else.

The world drifted away, the universe became this one man and their embrace.

She felt as if everything inside her were quivering, steadily working her into a rhythmic need that made her clench her thighs and start to roll her hips. Oh, man, she needed, wanted…

A woof startled her. She and Al separated quickly.

Hazy-eyed, with her lips feeling swollen, she turned her head and saw Bugle eyeing them quizzically.

"Oh, boy," said Al. "Jealous?"

"I'm not sure." She shook her head a little, trying to come back to reality, much as she didn't want to. She was, however, acutely aware of what this dog could do if he thought she was in trouble.

"Maybe," she said slowly, "it's his training. He's not supposed to let anyone touch me except casually."

Al snorted. "This could get fun."

"This could be maddening," she replied, regaining some of her sense of humor. "Now I've got to figure out how to let him know you're okay."

He laughed. "Are you sure that's wise?"

She liked the twinkle in his eyes, and the way he was taking this with humor. At that moment she wasn't very happy with Bugle. Interference at exactly the wrong time. Her body was still humming with the forces Al had awakened in her, but she had to deal with Bugle first. He probably wouldn't bite Al without a command, but he could easily insert himself between them as a matter of protection.

"Hmm," she said.

"Yeah," he answered.

"Bugle, it's okay."

He tilted his head the other way, as if trying to figure out this new and perplexing situation.

Kelly leaned slowly into Al's side and took his hand in hers. Bugle whimpered quietly. "It's okay," she said firmly.

He didn't budge, but his gaze was skimming over the entire situation.

"I should have asked Cadel for a command to tell him someone's a good person," she remarked dryly. "I could lock him in another room."

"I saw what he did to the door in your house. Nope, we gotta win him over. I have an idea."

He slid off the couch until he was on the floor. He reached out his hand, letting Bugle sniff him. "Now you come down here, too."

Kelly dropped to the floor beside him.

"Now start petting him like you're playing a little rough. When he seems happy I'll get in on the action with you."

Made sense, Kelly thought, but she never in her life would have imagined that she'd have to get her K-9's permission to make love. "Let me pull out his tennis ball, too. You can toss that for him a few times when he seems to be mellowing. That's his signal for playtime."

Al smiled. "He's not exactly *un*mellow right now. Just unsure."

She had several tennis balls in her tote, but brought out only one. She made a big ceremony of giving it to Al. Bugle was instantly engaged.

"Okay, big boy," she said, using both her hands to scratch around his neck, then playfully push him side to side. It took a minute or two, but soon he adopted the play posture, lowering his front legs until he rested on them. A happy woof escaped him.

She moved in for some more easy wrestling, and when Al joined her, Bugle didn't object. Soon he was bounding around the room and coming back to them both to nudge at them with his nose. Then Al threw the tennis ball.

And Bugle fell in love.

Kelly was laughing aloud at her dog's antics, and Al grinned from ear to ear. Bugle ran back with the ball and dropped it on Al. One more toss and he brought it back to give it to Kelly to throw. The bond was happening.

Eventually, Kelly fell back against the sofa, laughing, worn out from dog wrestling and ball tossing, as well as a long workday. She wasn't totally worn out by any means, but Bugle and Al had managed to ease her emotional turmoil.

Bugle could probably have kept at it for a long while, but he sensed the humans were done, so he returned to gnawing his rawhide as if it were all that existed on the planet.

Kelly looked over at Al and enjoyed the sight of him sprawled on his back on the floor. He seemed so relaxed now, the kind of relaxation

she'd seen in him before only when he was helping animals. He'd reached his place of serenity.

His position also revealed his body in a way
she'd never really noticed before. Oh, she'd always known he had a great build, but as he rested
there, she could see how deep and powerful his
chest was, how broad his shoulders and how incredibly flat his belly. Narrow hips, long legs
with thigh muscles that showed even through
his jeans…

He was a man in prime condition. Her heart
fluttered, and the heat he'd ignited in her renewed. Every cell in her body quivered with anticipation. If only he would roll over, reach for
her, touch her in places no one touched her. She
lost her breath just thinking about it. His hands
on her breasts, between her legs.

Oh, man, the bug had bit badly. She'd locked
away her womanly impulses for so long, acutely
aware that she was trying to make her way in
a man's world. In Fort Lauderdale, in Laramie,
there'd been plenty of guys ready to remind her
that she was "just a woman." There hadn't been
any of that here in Conard County, maybe because they'd long had female deputies, and two
of them were closely related to one of their most
prominent, Deputy Micah Parish. She was sure
nobody wanted to ever get on Micah's bad side.

But Sarah Ironheart and Connie Parish were
both related to him through marriage, one to

his brother, one to his son. Nope, they were accepted, all right, and that acceptance seemed to have extended to her and the few other women on the force. Connie hadn't always been a deputy, she recalled, but after Ethan joined the department, so had she. Then Ethan had left to help Micah with his ranch and Connie had remained.

Micah, she sometimes felt, was easing his way out of the department, working fewer hours, spending more time at home with Faith and their family. But with Micah, it was hard to be sure of anything.

And why was she thinking of him and his family, anyway? He was a solid man, an excellent deputy, and as far as she could tell blessed with both a deep spirituality and strong compassion.

None of that had anything to do with right now except that she was trying to divert herself before she did something incredibly forward, like jump Al's bones.

Her cheeks grew hot as she remembered saying that out loud, but she'd said it, and she'd meant it. And he'd called her wildly beautiful. Wow. That compliment reached all the way to her very core. Never once in her life had she ever felt that way about herself, nor had anyone ever told her that. But Al had, lifting her self-image in a new way.

Her thoughts were starting to drift to the frigid

night outside, and the missing girls. One maybe dead, but what about the others? She couldn't know. No one could. All they could do was hope and restart the search in the morning.

In the meantime, Al was right, she shouldn't dig herself into that hole. Right now it could do no good except ruin this entire night.

Al seemed to be watching the patterns the firelight and his Christmas tree made on the ceiling. The logs dulled the glow quite a bit but didn't entirely erase the dancing color. It all looked so warm.

And he looked so inviting.

Hardly aware of what she was doing, she pushed away from the couch and crawled across the floor toward him. She felt Bugle's eyes on her, then heard him resume his gnawing.

Al spoke. "If you're about to do what I think you're about to do, should we let the dog take a walk, first? He's already proved he has a talent for timely interruption."

He wasn't looking at her, but she could see the corners of his firm mouth twitch. In spite of the tension and excitement that filled her, she had to laugh. She loved that he could make her laugh.

"Probably," she answered, hearing the huskiness in her own voice.

To her surprise, he reached out and tugged her gently until she fell on his chest, then arranged her so she lay squarely on top of him. "I want you," he said boldly. "But the damn dog…"

Then he kissed her so hard and so deeply she felt as if he took possession of her very soul. Soon the niggling needs that had been tempting her with excited anticipation had become a wildfire of hunger.

"The dog," he said, tearing his mouth from hers. "Damn, do you feel good."

Then he rolled her gently to the side and rose to his feet in one smooth movement. "Bugle, walk."

Kelly tried to clear her throat and brain. "Business," she said.

Bugle at once dropped his rawhide bone and headed for the door where Al awaited him. A moment later he darted out into the frigid night.

"I bet he doesn't take long," Al remarked. "I think we've lost another ten or fifteen degrees. Must be on their way to Texas."

A thought that another time might have made her laugh, but right now impatience was riding her like a goad. If one more thing kept her from discovering what sex with Al was like, she might groan in frustration. She was hardly able to think of anything else at all. Unfortunately, he'd been right about the dog.

A few minutes later, a bark alerted them. Al opened the door and Bugle trotted in, a few snowflakes dotting his coat like diamonds. Then something else followed him at top speed.

"Regis?" Al said, disbelieving. "What the—"

Kelly sat up instantly. A gray squirrel had darted across the floor, then turned around and set himself up in the tiny Christmas tree.

It was too much. Bugle looked befuzzled, Al looked astonished and there was a gray squirrel sitting in an artificial tree amid the fiber-optic lighting.

Kelly started to laugh. Maybe it was hysterical laughter, but it felt damn good, and she wound up leaning against the couch and holding her sides. "Regis? What?"

"Exactly. What?" Al squatted and studied this new conundrum. "You didn't really want to go to bed with me tonight, did you?"

"I did."

"Well, we seem to have a whole bunch of busybodies here."

"Bugle will behave."

"I'm sure," Al retorted. "But Regis? I may have hand-raised him when he was orphaned last spring, but he's never been what I would call trained."

"So he doesn't have a family?"

"How would I know? He's been pretty much living as a free squirrel since I was able to release him last spring, but whether he hooked up with other squirrels, or had a family of his own,

I have no idea. He just shows up from time to time, like he wants to visit."

"Or maybe tonight is just too damn cold and you opened a warm door."

"Entirely possible." He sighed, then settled cross-legged on the floor. "I'd feel like a monster throwing him out if he's too cold but we *do* have a dog in here."

There was that inescapable fact. Just because she'd never seen Bugle chase squirrels or rabbits or anything like that didn't mean he wouldn't suddenly take a notion. "So you raised Regis, huh?"

"Well, I wasn't going to leave him to starve to death."

She was loving this view of Al. Hand-raising a squirrel? Letting the animal ride with him sometimes? The squirrel trusting enough to come inside even though there was a dog in here?

She looked at Bugle, who was still eyeing the animal as if unsure how to react. "Bugle, okay. Relax." *Relax* was a word she'd been using with him for the last few years and she had no idea if he grasped the concept. She was sure that dog understood more English than anyone realized, but she couldn't always be certain *which* words made sense and how he might interpret them.

Bugle shifted from one side to another, watching the squirrel, which seemed to be regarding him with at least some suspicion. He lowered himself slowly, reluctantly.

"Solution," said Al, rising. He walked out into his small kitchen and returned with a custard bowl full of sunflower seeds. "This'll keep Regis happy. As for Bugle…we could take him and his rawhide into the bedroom with us if you're still interested."

Still interested? She felt like a pot simmering on low heat, just waiting for the right time to boil. "Oh, yeah," she answered.

He smiled and held out his hand. "Not exactly the most romantic way to start out."

"I'm not looking for romance." And she wasn't. If there was ever to be any romance between them, it could come later. Tonight she wanted passion, fire and forgetfulness.

Bugle picked up his bone and followed them into the bedroom. Behind her, Kelly could hear the squirrel cracking sunflower seeds.

It was indeed as if she had entered a whole new world with Al, and when he drew her into his arms, she went with a leaping, eager heart. Had she spent all this time avoiding her attraction to him? Because it felt as if it had been deeply rooted in her forever.

Impatience was winning, however. They'd spent enough time dealing with dogs and then a squirrel. She wanted him and wanted him now before anything else happened.

He laughed quietly as she pulled at his shirt, and as their eyes met she saw both heat and delight in his gaze. He was as eager as she, and with every touch she seemed to lift out of herself until she felt she was floating in space.

Their clothes vanished, although she couldn't remember how and didn't especially care. At long last came the moment when they tumbled onto his bed in glorious nakedness, nothing left between them but bare skin.

The feeling of skin on skin was beyond compare, like nothing else in the world. She could feel the shackles of the everyday world letting go, could feel the freedom of being naked with a man and free to touch however she chose.

An amazing exuberance filled her, joining the growing heat that made her breasts ache and caused her to throb hungrily between her legs.

Running her hands over him, enjoying the way he moaned softly at her touches, she felt scars and signs of old injuries but ignored them for now. Nothing, absolutely nothing, was going to get in the way now. There would be later.

His small nipples were already hard, as hard as hers seemed to be, and she couldn't resist tonguing them and nipping gently, causing him to writhe and grab her shoulders. So much here to explore and discover. Sliding her hand down over his flat belly, she reached for his groin and found him stiff and ready, jerking at her lightest touch.

Excitement rushed through her, stronger than ever. She had wakened this in him. The sense of power and delight overwhelmed her.

She held him, stroking his silkiness softly, teasingly while she continued to torment the small buds of his nipples.

Then he apparently had enough.

He rolled her over and suddenly he was above her on his elbows, and the drowsy smile on his face promised more tortures to come. Tortures for her.

His tongue trailed over her neck, at first making it warm, then a chill followed, a delicious shiver. She'd never guessed her neck could respond that way. She grabbed his shoulders, feeling as if she would fall over a cliff edge if she didn't hang on for dear life.

Evidently he was as impatient as she, because soon he trailed his kisses to her breasts, sucking gently at first, then so hard she felt as if he were going to consume her. With each movement of his mouth, he sent another wave of desire racing through her, making her feel as if electric wires joined her breasts and her loins. Like being strung on a welder's arc, she burned for him.

His fingers found the sensitive nub between her legs, and at his first touch she learned that pain and pleasure could be the same. He rubbed her, his touches growing harder until her hips bucked helplessly, and moans escaped her. She had become a mindless bundle of need and want and he seemed to know it.

Then, at last, he slid over her and into her, filling her until everything inside her clenched with pleasure. Yesssssssss…

His thrusts were powerful, each one causing another happy moan to escape her. She felt as if he were pushing her, driving her ever higher into a world of magic, a place where stars exploded and filled the night with wonder.

Then came one last endless, almost painful moment when everything inside her seemed to pause in an infinite time of anticipation, where she almost feared she wouldn't tumble over the edge into satisfaction.

But with one last thrust, he brought her more pleasure and pain, the ecstasy of completion. Her world seemed to turn white like flame, and satisfaction rolled through her whole body like a powerful wave.

A cry escaped her, then him, and she felt him shudder as he followed her over the cliff into completion.

The world had slipped away, leaving her spent and happy, and secure in his arms. Nothing could be more perfect.

Chapter Twelve

The night passed too swiftly, yet not swiftly enough. Kelly slept better than she had any night since the teens disappeared, but even before the sun was up the anxiety began to fill her. The storm would arrive later today or early tomorrow. If they hoped to get any forensic evidence from where Misty had found that bone, this might be their only chance for a while.

The girls' lives might hinge on their speed.

Al appeared to feel pretty much the same. They'd managed to put the pizza in the fridge last night before it could spoil, and now he pulled it out. "Cold pie okay? I wanna start calling."

"Absolutely." Instead of feeding herself immediately, she took her bag into the bedroom and pulled out her fresh uniform. Bugle, who had spent the night at the foot of the bed, behaving himself, at once became alert. He loved to work.

Once she'd dressed and straightened herself up in his small bathroom, she emerged to smell coffee, to see a squirrel watching the world from his artificial tree and to hear Al on the phone. Now he was talking to Gage.

"It was Kelly's idea. She's thinking that Misty might remember where she found the bone, and I agree with her. Dogs don't lose their bones."

Gage must have agreed, because a minute later Al was on the phone with Misty's owners. It was early yet, but not as early as it might have been with the winter sun rising so late. The Avilas were agreeable to sharing their dog. They didn't know exactly why, and she gathered that Al had never mentioned the bone to them. They were, however, glad to do whatever they could to help with the search.

Good. They didn't need to be feeling uneasy around their dog because he'd been playing with a human bone. He was just a dog, making no moral connection to the idea of not disturbing a corpse.

They scarfed the pizza down with unseemly speed, and Al filled an insulated bottle with the fresh coffee before turning the pot off. Then he opened the door. "Out, Regis. You can't stay inside all day."

"Will he make a mess?" Kelly asked.

"He already has with those seed shells, but that's not what I'm worried about. He needs to be out doing squirrel things or I'll start to feel like I've deprived him of a real life by hand-raising him."

Kelly flashed a grin even as her stomach turned over nervously in anticipation of the day ahead. "You made sure he has a life. Right now he looks pretty happy."

But Regis was still a squirrel at heart, and with the door open he dashed out into the cold day. A wind had begun to batter the world, heralding the coming bad weather.

"I hope this storm doesn't show up earlier than expected," Kelly remarked as she pulled on her gloves and her watch cap.

"We'll do what we can. I'll catch up with you once I have Misty. The place where we found her?"

"Best place to start."

He caught her at the door before she could slip out and pressed a hard kiss on her mouth. "Later," he said. "Tonight."

Oh, she had no problem with that idea.

Bugle leaped up eagerly into his cage, and Kelly closed him in. He was going to need booties and his quilted vest today, she thought as the wind turned her cheeks almost instantly to ice.

It was a relief to climb into the cab of her truck and get out of the wind. She suspected the heater would take a while before it started blasting. Worse, she saw that snowflakes were falling again. Lightly. Almost like a promise more than a threat.

She had to face something, she realized as

she drove back to the place on the country road where she'd found Al trying to corral Misty: finding the remains might not tell them a damn thing.

She'd been hoping—she supposed everyone was still hoping—that they'd find the remains and find a clue. A clue as to what had happened, a clue as to who had done it. Would they? With a sinking stomach, she seriously feared they wouldn't learn a single useful thing, and maybe not in time to save the other girls even if they did. How long would forensics take?

No answers. They were racing into the teeth of a winter storm to gather evidence that might not save a single life. That might not help them find the perp.

This was the part of police work she most hated, finding evidence that didn't lead to the perp. Evidence that would be useful only once they found the baddie. Great in court, but no lighted road to the door of a killer or rapist.

Nor any guarantee that they would find something to lead them to the other girls, if the bone did indeed come from one of them. No guarantee they could save their lives.

No guarantees at all.

JANE AND CHANTAL huddled together beneath the stinking blankets. Upon awakening, Jane had remarked that there was more food and water.

The thinnest stream of light that came through a crack in the boards over the window had become, for the girls, almost as bright as a midday sun. It was the only light they ever saw, and somehow they adapted.

They found, too, that they'd each had one hand released from the chains. They used the slightly increased mobility to double the blankets and give themselves a little more warmth in their cocoon as they downed the power bars with the aid of water. Neither of them cared anymore if the water was drugged. Sleep was now preferable to wakefulness.

"We're never going to get out of here," Jane said.

"We can't be sure." But in all honesty, Chantal figured she was going to die in this hole. All eating and drinking did was forestall the inevitable. But she didn't want to say that to Jane. Having both of them suicidally depressed would help nothing at all.

She pushed up as best she could to pick out the place where they'd stuffed strands of yarn from her bright green sweater. Only one strand appeared to be left in the crack. Not enough to be seen by anyone.

"Finish that bar," she said wearily to Jane. "We're going to unravel some more of my sweater, make a bigger flag to shove out there."

Jane merely sighed, as if an answer required

more strength than she had. Minutes passed before she appeared to find energy to reply. "You tear down that sweater too much and you're going to freeze to death." She paused. "It doesn't matter, does it?"

"Of course it matters or I wouldn't be trying. We're going to make this as big as we can fit into that crack. This color ought to stand out like neon." The winter countryside now was so washed out with shades of winter brown and gray-green that any bright color ought to catch attention. She pulled at the yarn, trying to gather her exhausted thoughts into an idea of what to do with this to make it more noticeable. That crack, after all, wasn't very big. Long streamers had evidently been pulled out by the wind. So maybe a big ball to anchor them. She yanked more yarn out of the sweater.

Then Jane caused a new and different kind of chill to run through Chantal. "When he brought this last water and food, I saw his face. If we could get out, I could identify him."

Chantal stared blindly into the near darkness, her fingers growing still. If he hadn't concealed his face, he meant for them to die here. She'd begun to suspect it but facing the reality made her quail deep inside. She didn't want to die. She was only eighteen. There were so many things she had always wanted to do. A tear burned in her eye, but it was wasteful and she was almost perpetually dehydrated in the icy air, despite the water bottles. The tear never escaped and she sought to stabilize her reeling emotions. "Jane?"

"Yeah. I know. God help me, if I get a chance…"

"Who is he?"

"We saw him playing pool at the tavern with another guy. I could point him out. I could describe him. So could you. He was the shorter one."

Chantal flashed back to what had since become the last happy moments of her short life, and she did indeed remember. Ick. What a creep! Was she going to let him win?

Sudden strength infused her limbs and she started pulling at the yarn of her sweater once again. "We're going to get out of here, Jane. Our parents won't quit. They won't let anyone quit. We'll get out of here if I have to knit us booties for our feet with my teeth. But right now we need to poke out the biggest flag I can put together. Someone will see it because I swear they haven't stopped looking."

"Maybe not," Jane said tiredly. "Mary Lou…"

"We can't afford to think about her now. I'm afraid…"

"Me, too." Jane fell silent, then said, "Want me to try to braid some of those strands?"

"Good idea. The wind's probably getting strong enough to blow them around. Let's make them longer and fatter."

As she ruthlessly ripped yarn from her sweater into long lengths, she sawed it with her teeth to separate it so Jane could braid it.

"I never imagined," Jane muttered, "that braiding my horse's mane for the county fair would come in useful."

Under any other circumstances, Chantal would have laughed. But some creep had stolen her laughter. She wanted it back.

THE CREEP IN question had closed the shutters over the windows of his ramshackle house to better withstand the coming storm. He pulled his pickup into the lean-to that would provide some shelter. He'd already stocked up on supplies, and even had extra thanks to all the energy bars and water he'd bought for those girls. So if he got snowed in and for some reason lost the use of his water pump, he'd be fine.

And they'd be dead.

Crazy, he thought. He'd wanted to make them his slaves, to whip them into line and make them serve him in any way he decided. Now they were going to die because of Spence's stupidity and a coming storm that would probably suck the last life out of them with its cold.

He ought to be furious. Instead he only felt two things: fear that he might have left evidence on that stuffed rabbit he'd overlooked, and a strangely warm feeling about those girls dying.

Odd, he'd been mad when he killed the first one. She'd infuriated him and gotten her just deserts. He hadn't felt then what he was feeling now: a kind of pleasurable delight not unlike sex.

Those two girls would die on his say-so because he refused to set them free. They were totally at his mercy, and he liked that. Although he could have let them out, he supposed. They'd die quickly enough in their thin clothes with nothing but slipper socks on their feet. He'd made sure that they had no warm winter gear for protection.

Once that storm started howling, he could throw them out into its fury and let it erase them until long after they were dead. By the time anyone found them, they'd probably be as chewed up as the one he'd already tossed aside. He kind of liked that image, too. On the other hand, forcing them to lie in that basement and just die because he *wouldn't* let them go appealed to him even more. *He* was the man in charge, in charge of something more important than shoveling manure and fixing old cars for the first time in his life.

A few nights ago he hadn't been able to resist visiting the body of the first girl. He wanted to see what the animals and elements had done to her. Bones had been tossed about, little flesh was left at all, and the only thing that caught his eye was a small gold necklace with a cross that he'd missed at the outset.

He considered taking it, then decided it didn't matter anymore if they identified the body.

They wouldn't be able to trace it to him. Let her family have that stupid keepsake…if they ever found the body.

He was sitting there, enjoying a longneck, patting himself on his back mentally, thinking just how smart he was.

Then there was a hammering at his door.

MISTY FOUND THE BONES, all right. At first she seemed to have no interest in helping, as if she couldn't understand what they expected of her. But then Kelly decided it was worth a try and retrieved the target bags. The bags containing pieces of clothing from the girls. Just maybe Misty would remember the scent and along with it the bones, although her hopes weren't really high.

"The cadaver dogs didn't find anything," she remarked to Al as she zipped the bags closed. "Why should Misty?"

"Maybe the cadaver dogs didn't get close enough." He shrugged one shoulder as Gage joined them. A line of searchers, already looking cold, edged the road again.

"I think," Gage said, "that it's time we got some luck on this. By the way, that rabbit left at your place? I sent it to the lab for forensics. Something not right about any of that."

"Tell me," Al said dryly.

"Okay, let's see what Misty can do for us. Maybe Bugle can follow the scent."

"I don't know," Kelly answered honestly. "Misty may remember she smelled it before when she found the bone. Bugle wouldn't be able to track it from here unless the victim passed this way."

"Good point." Gage shook his head. The last three weeks seemed to have aged him. "All right. Go for it, Al."

Misty suddenly became eager. Maybe she wanted to get back to her toys. Maybe she just wanted an excuse to run around the countryside. Only time would tell.

The rest of the searchers were told to keep back about twenty feet in case something turned up. They didn't want the scents to become muddied.

For a while it seemed as if Misty was prancing around the field as she had the day Al had found her with the bone. But Misty had her own methods of operation, and eventually the dancing gave way to a more directed movement. She *did* seem to know where she was going.

Kelly followed a little more closely with Bugle but was careful not to get in the way in case Misty made a discovery. Behind her, crime scene techs were ready to get to work, the sooner the better given the increasingly bitter cold.

Then Misty came upon the remains, over two miles in from a county road, in a gully now filled with tumbleweed. She jumped around, then wanted to dive in, but Al restrained her with a powerful arm.

Bugle walked a little closer and announced with a whimper that he recognized the odor. At once he sat at attention.

There was nothing left, Kelly thought as the team cautiously pulled away the tumbleweed. Nothing but some hair. Not even a scrap of cloth. Teeth and DNA would probably be necessary for ID, and the bones were pretty well scattered around.

Gage stood at the edge of the gully for long moments, then said, "My God, I recognize that cross." He looked up, closed his eyes and appeared to steel himself. "Mary Lou."

A HALF HOUR LATER, Kelly felt so helpless and hopeless she could barely stand it. Bugle kept pulling her west, toward another county road, as if he was after something. Finally, she decided to give him his head.

"Bugle scents something. I'm going to let him lead."

Gage nodded. "Go."

Al, who was still hanging on to a disappointed Misty, looked as if he wanted to go with her.

"Take Misty home," she said. "You'll be able

to find me at the road out there. How far will I go without my truck?"

"Give me your keys. I'll bring it to you after I return Misty."

She watched him and the dog trot away, then looked at Bugle. "I hope you know what you're doing."

Because it was utterly unlikely that girl had gotten here under her own steam. If she had, there'd at least have been some patches of cloth left.

Bugle put his nose to the ground but after about five yards lifted it, indicating that whatever he was looking for was in the air.

It never ceased to amaze her that dogs could detect odors up to three hundred feet above their heads, and odors that might be weeks old, even in the air. The dang air was moving all the time, right?

But maybe he wasn't getting the scent out of the air. There was enough dry grass and brush around to have caught those odors and retain them even through the cold they'd been having. Or maybe some of the predators that had gotten to Mary Lou's body had left their own trail and he was following *them*.

Sometimes she really, truly wished Bugle could talk. She'd have loved to question him for hours about how he perceived the world.

But he was on a determined trek, and since

she couldn't do anything back at the body, she might as well keep following. As the sky grew more leaden, and the wind stiffer, it occurred to her that once Al caught up to her with her truck, she could perhaps do one more swing of welfare checks along this road.

There'd been enough badness over the last few weeks. They didn't need people dying in this storm.

The hike was fairly long, well over a couple of miles before they reached the crossroad, but at least the quick pace of the walk was helping to keep her warm. She wondered if Bugle was glad of his quilted vest or if it annoyed him. But these temperatures must be as dangerous to him as to anyone else. In one of her pockets she'd tucked his booties in case it started to snow heavily. Right now he was okay, but if ice started to build up between his toes, he wouldn't be.

Not that there was any danger of that yet. Snowflakes were in the air, but so light it hardly seemed possible a killer storm was headed in over those mountains.

At last they reached the road, but Bugle wasn't done. He tugged her to the right and she followed, after closing the sagging ranch gate behind her. She just wished she knew what he was after. She guessed she'd find out when he discovered it.

So much of this county looked all the same—

ranchlands and fences and wide-open vistas until you ran up against the mountains—that if she hadn't known which county road she was trotting along, she might have been anywhere.

But then something caught her eye. Something she remembered about the way the road looked. Too recently familiar. Hadn't she stopped here the other day? Somewhere just up ahead?

At that moment, Bugle came to a halt. Full stop. He sat, telling her he'd found it. She stared at him, then looked around, trying to figure it out until she remembered.

The glove.

The *glove*.

This was where they'd found that glove, and he'd tracked it from Mary Lou's remains. Her heart began to race and her stomach tried to flip over. A connection. No way to know what it meant, but it was a connection according to Bugle, and she absolutely couldn't afford to ignore it when he was doing his job.

She had yet to see him make a mistake when it came to his olfactory sense. This dog said that body was linked to this spot where the glove had been found.

Pulling off her own glove, she reached under her parka for her radio and called.

AL HEARD KELLY'S radio call shortly after he returned Misty to her owners and expressed his gratitude. He offered them absolutely no idea of the grisly task she'd been asked to perform; let them think she'd helped him round up another dog.

They wanted to talk about the storm, but he eased away from that, just warning them not to let Misty out off her lead.

"If she decides to go for a run, I may not have time to find her."

He looked at the kids, the usual aides to Houdini-dog, and they nodded solemnly with wide eyes.

He picked up Kelly's truck, leaving his own behind, and headed out to the county road where he'd promised to meet her. So Bugle had tracked the glove all the way from the remains. Although she didn't mention the body directly, only that he'd followed the trail from where she'd started her walk. Damn, dogs were amazing.

Not that this was going to tell them enough to find the other girls or the kidnapper. But it was still an essential link.

He listened to the chatter. Gage asked Kelly to flag the location and said he'd send some deputies out her way if she found anything else. Right now they were busy searching the current area for other signs.

"So far," Gage said irritably, "our dogs have found two raccoons and a fox. Yee-haw."

"Must have had a fight over the body," someone else remarked.

"Not on the air," Gage snapped. "How many police scanners do we have in this county? Keep it all under your hat. Face-to-face or shut up."

All that skirting around the word *body* and someone had blown it with one statement. Al might have been amused under other circumstances. There was nothing amusing about this.

When he caught up with Kelly, she was standing by the road and the pin flags she'd used to mark the spot Bugle had led her to. They might not survive the storm, probably wouldn't, but he was sure she'd marked the GPS coordinates and saved them. Routine for her.

He offered to let her drive as she piled Bugle into his cage and into the warmth of the SUV. She shook her head and climbed into the passenger seat.

"I am so *cold* I'm not sure my fingers could manage the steering wheel," she said as she fumbled at the seat belt clasp. "Dang, that dog dragged me quite a distance in this icy weather. Three miles? Maybe more? He seems fine, though."

"Well, he *does* have that quilted vest."

"It's not like I'm running around out here naked," she answered a bit tartly. "Damn, Al. The glove. The body. So they're linked but where do they get us?"

"That the glove fell off a truck and Bugle says it was near the body. That's good for something."

"You'd think. But *who*?"

Which, of course, was the big question.

He let the vehicle idle, blowing heat into the compartment, while neither of them said a word. He suspected they were both trying to figure out what this could mean. That the kidnapper lived somewhere along this road? Or that he'd just driven through here? Hardly a guided tour of his whereabouts.

"I was thinking of driving out along here for a final welfare check," Kelly said after a few minutes. "Might as well since I'm here. But could you drive? Slowly? I want to use my binoculars to scan the countryside. Just because I didn't notice anything a few days ago doesn't mean nothing is out there. I saw a tumbledown line shack that's probably empty, but there's another house up this way a few miles. Maybe the guy noticed something."

Without a word, Al put the SUV in gear. Unlike many vehicles, it proved to be capable of moving at five miles an hour. Kelly kept her binoculars pasted to her eyes. Big binoculars, the kind he used to carry. Those long lenses could see a long way.

"Just don't hit a rut," she muttered.

Yeah, it would jam those eyepieces into the bones around her eyes. An unpleasant experience.

Then all of a sudden she said sharply, "Stop!"

He obeyed, trying not to ram the binoculars into her eyes. The instant the vehicle stopped rolling, she hopped out and resumed scanning the countryside.

He put the vehicle in Park and locked the brake before climbing out to join her. "What did you see?"

"I thought I saw something like chartreuse. There's nothing that should be that color out here."

"Where?"

She lowered the binoculars and pointed. "Believe it or not, near the base of the line shack."

"Oh, that's not a line shack," he said as he began to scan the area she indicated, adjusting the focus to make the building even larger to his eye. "Old ranch house. Man, somebody must have abandoned it two generations ago. It was tiny! Nobody could…"

His voice trailed off as his gaze fixated.

"Al?"

"I see it, too. It looks like some fabric poking out of a boarded-up window."

"Then let's go."

He lowered the binoculars, eyed the terrain and figured they might be lucky to have suspension after this drive. Lucky if their axles weren't broken. "It's going to be rough." It also might be a humongous waste of time, although at this point it was beginning to feel like wasting time was all they were going to do, anyway.

"All right, let's go. And put your gloves back on. You need those fingers."

He could sense Kelly's impatience in the way she leaned forward against her seat belt, but she didn't press him to a higher speed. She evidently was as aware as he that Bugle was in the back and didn't want him to be banged around inside his cage.

Steadily, with plenty of stomach-dropping dips and jaw-jolting rocks, they approached the shack.

And there was no question but what something green was fluttering from a boarded-up window. Detritus blown there by the wind? Maybe, but it looked more purposeful.

This time Kelly leaped out before the vehicle fully stopped and ran toward the fluttering green strands. She leaned her face toward it and called loudly, "Girls? Are you in there? Is anyone in there?"

The wind almost snatched her words away, but he heard the response of faint cries.

"We're coming in to get you out. Sheriff."

Well, that settled that, Al thought. He couldn't even begin to describe the feelings that twisted up his insides. Good. Bad. Relief.

God help them. He feared they'd find nothing good.

Going round to the other side of the shack,

he found the cellar doors, heavy steel, chained and padlocked.

"Kelly," he said, "I'm going to use my gun. Call the sheriff to send an ambulance and more help while I open this up."

Then, standing to one side and hoping a ricochet merely bounced away into the weeds, he fired at the padlock.

He heard faint screams from inside, but he had to get this damn thing open. If he'd had his own truck, he'd have had bolt cutters. But he didn't, and his gun it was going to have to be.

"One more time," he shouted, hoping that was all it would take.

Kelly came round. "Help is on the way. We could wait but I'm not sure..."

He agreed. More than anything, those girls needed to be freed. They probably needed a lot of other things, like medical help, but primarily they needed to know they were safe now.

He leveled his gun again and took another shot at the lock. This time, probably with the help of the cold, it shattered and released the chain.

Kelly beat him down the steps. He listened to girls sob. And he waited for the sirens.

They had the teens. Now they just had to find their tormentor. He went to Kelly's SUV and hunted up the blankets he was sure she must carry for use at accident scenes. When he found them, he took them downstairs and fought back a wave of fury as he saw the girls' condition. Scarecrows. Filthy scarecrows.

It had been a while since he'd killed anyone, but he wanted to kill right now.

Then he heard Chantal's friend say, "I know who took us."

Chapter Thirteen

Day 22

Walton Revell tried to blame the kidnapping on his friend Spencer. There was the stuffed rabbit, after all. Jane defeated him, however, because she'd seen him.

And when he was arraigned before Judge Wyatt Carter and looked into the black gaze of Al Carstairs, he knew he was peering into hell. For the first time it occurred to him that he might be safer in prison than in walking away from the sheriff.

He was remanded into federal custody for the kidnapping, but there were also charges of murder and attempted murder, and a whole bunch of other things that added up to false imprisonment and torture. Maybe some other stuff, too, but the feds would put him away for life, whether the state decided to pursue the other charges. His public defender, who looked as if she'd be happy to kill him herself, didn't hold out much hope.

Not even a plea bargain.

Finally, Walton Revell began to wonder what had possessed him and why he'd ever thought this would be a good idea. All he'd done was end his own freedom, not make slaves out of the girls.

Now he'd be a slave to someone inside the pen. *Great thinking, idiot.*

At least he had the pleasure of seeing Spence have to explain why he'd put the rabbit in Kelly Noveno's house. "She was taking too long," Spence answered simply. "They weren't finding them girls. I admit I took it out of the car when I saw it along the road, but I got mad when she wouldn't answer my questions about the investigation and I decided to give her a scare. Speed her up."

He got a B&E for entering her house. The county attorney said there might be additional charges, like interfering with evidence, but no one seemed in much of a rush to hang Spence. No, Spence was all too eager to hang Reve, ready to talk about how they'd often discussed what it would be like to have some women as slaves.

He thought they were just kidding around.

Apparently, Reve hadn't been.

LEGS AND HANDS SHACKLED, Reve was led out toward a cell. The FBI would be coming to get him as soon as the blizzard passed. Yeah, the same

FBI who hadn't shown much interest until they got word the arrest was made.

"Better late than never," Kelly remarked.

"Well, we didn't have a heckuva lot to go on when we first contacted them," Gage said. "I'm more interested in what they'll do now."

The storm had arrived. The outside world looked dangerous and bleak, but Al insisted Kelly and Bugle come to his place. He could tell she was dragging anchor, as if someone had let the air out of a balloon that had been over-inflated.

He had some idea of how she'd been beating herself up, but now that could stop. The girls' families were with them at the hospital, and he told Kelly they'd go visit once the storm passed and it was possible to move around again.

She simply nodded. He was sure she was thinking of the lost Mary Lou, but there wasn't a thing that could be done about that.

At his place he barely unlocked the door before Regis darted in, but he didn't come alone. He had a bunch of smaller squirrels with him. His kids? Who knew. He brought out a bigger bowl of sunflower seeds and a small bowl of water and let them take up residence in his Christmas tree.

Bugle found his rawhide bone, ignored the squirrels and settled down to a happy chew. Kelly was the only one who couldn't seem to settle. She changed from her uniform into a set of flannel pajamas, a royal blue fuzzy robe and slippers and looked comfortable.

But nothing about her felt comfortable.

He made coffee, pulled out the leftover pizza and a Danish he'd bought a couple of days ago, and motioned her to eat something.

"I've got cereal and soup, too," he offered.

"This is fine." She took a mug of steaming coffee, then sat and ate two whole pieces of cold pizza. The weather and stress had made her hungry.

Heck, everything was making him hungry, too. Without apology to himself or the world, he pulled out a package of chocolate chip cookies and opened it, dumping them in a bowl. Then he sliced himself a huge piece of Danish and dug in.

Sitting beside her on the couch, he said, "I can think of no one else on this planet I would rather be snowbound with."

That snapped her into the present. A smile began to play over her lips. "Truly?"

"Truly." He just hoped he could trust himself now, but the last few weeks had made him believe in his ability to control himself around Kelly. No out-of-control rages, no desires to smash something other than that kidnapping creep. Being around her made him feel centered.

KELLY FELT HER heart skip a few beats, then begin to rise as it hadn't risen much since the disappearance of those girls. Their kidnapping had drained most of the joy from her life, except last night in Al's arms. She wanted to know that feeling again.

Just past him she could see out the windows. He hadn't drawn the heavy curtains yet, and the blizzard was now concealing the whole world. They were locked away together for at least the next day if not longer. Her gaze trailed back to him, and she saw something new in his expression, something she hadn't seen before: hope.

"I know what I told you about me and relationships," he continued. "It might still be true, but there's only one way to find out. I've enjoyed all the time I've spent with you over the last few weeks, and I didn't get triggered, at least not much. So it's possible…if you're willing to try. Kelly, will you date me? Formally. Like movies, and dinners, and maybe…some cohabitation while we try it on?"

As if her face had been frozen for three weeks, she felt a smile crack her cheeks, almost painful in its intensity. "Yes," she said simply.

"Yes to what?"

"To dating, to cohabiting…at least if you think your squirrels can live with my dog."

His face brightened as if the sun was rising on it. Outside a storm raged, but inside peace had settled.

"I think we can all get along. Besides, Regis has his own drey if he doesn't like it here."

She glanced toward the Christmas tree, where about four squirrels seemed to be sleeping. "I think *they* like it here. I know I do."

Then, throwing the stress of weeks, along with all doubts and fears, out into the storm, she wound her arms around him and looked deeply into his eyes. "You won't escape easily, Carstairs."

"I don't want to, Noveno."

Then they dissolved into laughter and fell on the floor, rolling together and hanging on tightly. The animals left them alone.

It was happy time for people.

* * * * *

Don't forget previous titles in Rachel Lee's Conard County: The Next Generation series:

Conard County Watch
Conard County Revenge
Undercover in Conard County
Conard County Marine
Conard County Spy

Available now from
Harlequin Romantic Suspense!

Get 4 FREE REWARDS!

We'll send you 2 FREE Books plus 2 FREE Mystery Gifts.

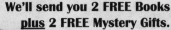

Harlequin® Romantic Suspense books feature heart-racing sensuality and the promise of a sweeping romance set against the backdrop of suspense.

FREE Value Over **$20**

Get 4 FREE REWARDS!

We'll send you 2 FREE Books
plus 2 FREE Mystery Gifts.

Harlequin Presents® books feature a sensational and sophisticated world of international romance where sinfully tempting heroes ignite passion.

FREE
Value Over
$20

Get 4 FREE REWARDS!

We'll send you 2 FREE Books plus 2 FREE Mystery Gifts.

FREE Value Over $20

Both the **Romance** and **Suspense** collections feature compelling novels written by many of today's best-selling authors.

YES! Please send me 2 FREE novels from the Essential Romance or Essential Suspense Collection and my 2 FREE gifts (gifts are worth about $10 retail). After receiving them, if I don't wish to receive any more books, I can return the shipping statement marked "cancel." If I don't cancel, I will receive 4 brand-new novels every month and be billed just $6.74 each in the U.S. or $7.24 each in Canada. That's a savings of at least 16% off the cover price. It's quite a bargain! Shipping and handling is just 50¢ per book in the U.S. and 75¢ per book in Canada.* I understand that accepting the 2 free books and gifts places me under no obligation to buy anything. I can always return a shipment and cancel at any time. The free books and gifts are mine to keep no matter what I decide.

Choose one: ☐ **Essential Romance** (194/394 MDN GMY7)   ☐ **Essential Suspense** (191/391 MDN GMY7)

Name (please print)

Address   Apt. #

City   State/Province   Zip/Postal Code

> Mail to the **Reader Service:**
> **IN U.S.A.:** P.O. Box 1341, Buffalo, NY 14240-8531
> **IN CANADA:** P.O. Box 603, Fort Erie, Ontario L2A 5X3

Want to try 2 free books from another series? Call 1-800-873-8635 or visit www.ReaderService.com.